THE RA[NCHER'S]
BABY PROPOSAL

———

Barbara White Daille

HARLEQUIN® WESTERN ROMANCE

Recycling programs
for this product may
not exist in your area.

ISBN-13: 978-0-373-75759-6

The Rancher's Baby Proposal

Printed in U.S.A.

Reagan wrapped his free arm around Ally and took her mouth.

It was firm and soft, molding to his. She nestled her body against his as if they'd been made to go together.

He was determined to have the pleasure of seeing all of her, and though he tried to slow it down, anticipation speeded things up.

The colors in the fabric seemed to blend together as he undid her buttons. The sight of pink lace beneath her blouse made his hand shake. She traced his knuckles with her fingertips as if guiding him, urging him on.

"Reagan," she murmured, "do you know how many times I've thought about us like this?"

He kissed her temple. "Not as many as I have lately."

"Oh, I doubt that." She laughed, low and sexy. His fingers fumbled on a button. "I've had a crush on you forever."

He kissed her cheek. "Forever, huh?"

"Mmm-hmm. But I've always known this would happen someday. And I'm happy it finally has."

He smiled. "I'm hoping I can make you even happier..."

Dear Reader,

In many of my stories, the heroes and heroines have known each other in the past and have a shared history. In the case of the reunion in *The Rancher's Baby Proposal*, I'm afraid the history is a little one-sided.

Ally Martinez grew up crushing on "older boy" Reagan Chance, Cowboy Creek's high school sports hero. Now Reagan is back, and at long last, he wants Ally—for his son's babysitter! Though she has never been comfortable around kids, knowing Reagan needs help makes her take the job. And very soon, love in is the air...between Ally and Reagan's baby. The situation between the two adults is another story.

Reagan was badly hurt by the ex who rejected him and his infant son. He's determined not to fall in love again. A one-night stand isn't the answer for either Reagan or Ally. Yet she's a complex, loving woman who cares for his son. And he's finding it hard to stay away from her...

If you're a frequent visitor to Cowboy Creek and the Hitching Post Hotel, I hope you enjoy dropping in again! If you're a first-time visitor, no worries. Each book stands alone with its own happy-ever-after ending.

I would love to hear from you any time at my website, barbarawhitedaille.com, or my mailing address: PO Box 504, Gilbert, AZ 85299.

All my best to you.

Until we meet again,

Barbara White Daille

Barbara White Daille and her husband still inhabit their own special corner of the wild, wild Southwest, where the summers are long and hot and the lizards and scorpions roam.

Barbara loves looking back at the short stories and two books she wrote in grade school and realizing that—except for the scorpions—she's doing exactly what she planned. She has now hit double digits with published novels and still has a file drawer full of stories to be written.

As always, Barbara hopes you will enjoy reading her books! She would love to have you drop by for a visit at her website, barbarawhitedaille.com.

Books by Barbara White Daille

Harlequin Western Romance

The Hitching Post Hotel

The Cowboy's Little Surprise
A Rancher of Her Own
The Lawman's Christmas Proposal
Cowboy in Charge
The Cowboy's Triple Surprise

Harlequin American Romance

The Sheriff's Son
Court Me, Cowboy
Family Matters
A Rancher's Pride
The Rodeo Man's Daughter
Honorable Rancher
Rancher at Risk

Visit the Author Profile page
at Harlequin.com for more titles.

To the original fabulous four of the Writers' Block and, of course, to Rich.

Chapter One

Ally Martinez had begun to doubt she would ever find an eligible cowboy.

In the small-parts aisle of Cowboy Creek Hardware and Feed, she knelt on the unvarnished pine flooring and tried to keep from muttering aloud. After all these years of separating nuts from bolts from washers, hauling bags of feed and restocking spools of twine, she was still as unattached as the day she had begun working here.

It wasn't as if she had taken the job after high school specifically to find a man. It wasn't even that she was eager to get married—or to have a brand-new baby, the way her best friend, Tina, had just done. Babies and she didn't get along. At the touch of her hand, they somehow read her inexperience and knew they didn't want to have anything to do with her.

No, it wasn't any of the above that made her long to find a cowboy. She simply wanted someone special in her life. And lucky for her since she lived in ranch country, she had always been partial to men who looked good in jeans and a Stetson.

"What's up with you, girl?" a familiar male voice asked. "You look like you just lost your best friend."

She sprang to her feet and wiped her dusty hands on her jeans. Smiling, she turned to face the tall, white-haired man standing at the end of the aisle. "*You'd* better not have lost her, Jed, since I left you in charge of her and the baby."

"I sure hope that little one doesn't pick up any of your sauciness, young lady." Even as Tina's grandfather pretended to scowl at her, he laughed. They knew each other well. In his seventies now, Jed Garland had semiretired but still oversaw the running of Garland Ranch. He definitely stayed on top of things when it came to the Hitching Post, his family-owned hotel on the same property.

"How are Mama and baby?" she asked as she approached him. "Did they get discharged from the hospital today, as planned?"

"They sure did." He beamed. "Cole brought them both home earlier this morning."

"Great. Can I come visit tonight?"

"Now, since when do you have to ask? The Hitching Post is your second home. You're free tonight?"

"Well…" He would expect a teasing response. Everyone expected lightheartedness from Ally Martinez, whose senior high school claim to fame was being voted The Girl Most Likely to Make You Laugh. "I do have lots of options, Jed. I could hang out at the Bowl-a-Rama, the Big Dipper or SugarPie's. Except I don't feel like bowling, don't have a taste for ice cream and certainly don't need any of Sugar's famous desserts." Grinningly wryly, she patted her "generous" hips, as Mama called them.

"Of course, there's always the Cantina," he said.

She nodded. On many Fridays and Saturdays, she

spent her nights at the only restaurant in Cowboy Creek, New Mexico, with both a bar and a dance floor. "You know I love to dance. But truthfully—" and she certainly did mean it "—tonight, I'll be thrilled to see Tina and the baby instead."

"Good. I'll tell her to expect you."

He turned to leave, then suddenly took a step backward. "Sorry, young man, I almost stampeded you."

From where she stood in the aisle, she could see only the brim of a worn Stetson and the shoulder and arm of a man wearing a T-shirt as snug as her jeans. Wrapped around that biceps, though, snug looked good.

"Well, I'll be," Jed said, sounding delighted. "Reagan Chase, great to see you again."

Ally's heart skipped a beat. Her thoughts began to race. Was it really Reagan, the boy who had left town seven years ago and left her with a broken heart? Was she going to pass out right here in the nuts-and-bolts aisle of the store?

What, and let him know how much seeing him again had affected her? Not in *her* lifetime.

Instead, she called up her usual response when life threw something bad or sad or uncomfortable her way. She pasted on a smile and pretended it didn't matter.

She reacted just in time, as Reagan stepped into view and reached out to shake Jed's hand. Reagan's shoulders had gotten broader since she had last seen him. He'd grown taller, too. His hand looked firm and strong... and tanned. She wouldn't have expected that from a man—a boy—who had left his hometown to go away to college in the city.

"What are you doing in Cowboy Creek?" Jed asked.

"I came back to take care of business."

Reagan's voice had also changed over the years. It had always been deep but now sounded hollow, too, with a serious tone she didn't recognize.

"It's been a while since my dad died," he continued, "and it's time to sell the ranch. You know our place as well as anyone does, Jed. If you hear of somebody looking for a spread that size, I'd appreciate it if you would share the info and pass my name along to them."

"I'm happy to do that for you, of course. But I had always hoped you'd come back and work the ranch yourself someday. I know your mama and daddy looked forward to that, too."

Ally held her breath, waiting for Reagan's response. His family's ranch was the only tie he had left to Cowboy Creek. If he sold that...

But he didn't respond to Jed's question. Instead, he turned his head and spotted her standing like a common eavesdropper in the small-parts aisle.

"Ally." He removed his Stetson and nodded, giving her a brief smile. It was nothing like the broad grin she had loved since grade school and seen less and less often during their high school days. His face looked drawn, lined with fatigue. Her heart thumped. Was he ill?

"I'd best be getting along," Jed said. He clapped Reagan on the shoulder. "Son, you stop by and visit us at the Hitching Post, y'hear me?"

Reagan nodded. "I will."

Jed ambled away. Reagan stood looking at her. She stared back, fighting to find something to say. In an instant, she had returned to being the gawky teenager dying for the older boy's attention. She had never gotten it back then. Now that she had it, she didn't know how to respond.

Pull yourself together, that's how.

"Hi, Reagan," she said, hoping he couldn't hear the slight tremor of excitement in her voice. "I…I heard what you said to Jed. I'm sorry you're thinking of selling your ranch."

"Not thinking of it. Doing it. As soon as I can get the place cleared out enough to put it up for sale."

His parents had lived their entire married lives in the house on that ranch. Reagan had lived there, too, until he had gone away to school. There must be so many memories wrapped up in the property…and so many personal items in the house. He would need a while to get it ready to sell. Meanwhile, would he spend that time here in Cowboy Creek? She crossed her fingers.

He gestured down the aisle. "Taking care of some shopping?"

"Oh. No. I'm not much of a do-it-yourselfer. I work here, have worked here since I graduated five years ago." By that point, he had already left town. After getting his degree, rumor had it, he had accepted a fancy job in the big city of Houston, Texas. Smiling, she shrugged. "I'm still only a small-town girl who replaced school with a dead-end job paying barely above minimum wage. But who's complaining?"

He looked at her thoughtfully. "Do you get any time off?"

Her stomach fluttered as if a dozen butterflies had taken wing inside her. Sad. She had just acknowledged she was no longer a schoolgirl. She should also no longer be prey to her feelings for the boy she had once loved. And yet, she couldn't tamp down her excitement.

"Yes, I get evenings off. I only work seven to three. And once in a while I have a free day during the week, when I have to work Saturday. But that's not too often."

His mouth curved into a small, one-sided smile. "It's almost three now. If you don't have any plans for right after work, would you be able to meet me at SugarPie's for a cold drink?"

"Yes." Her voice cracked. She hid her nerves behind a cough. "My throat's very dry. I could definitely use a cold drink." But none of Sugar's delicious desserts.

It didn't matter. With Reagan sitting across from her, she would get all she needed of something sweet.

ONCE HE ARRIVED at SugarPie's, Reagan found a reception committee waiting for him. At midafternoon, the sandwich shop wasn't that busy, but the customers, the waitress and even Sugar herself had greeted him the moment he'd walked in.

As the crowd surrounded him, a wave of memories seemed to engulf him, too. These were all friends of his, friends of his folks' and, for a moment, it felt like the old days before he'd left Cowboy Creek. For another, longer moment, he wished he could turn back the clock, change history, erase some of the things he had said and done…

Except for becoming a daddy. He would never regret having his son.

The crowd all welcomed him home, asking friendly questions he felt grateful he could answer with simple responses. He spoke to everyone in turn, shook hands with the men and gave hugs to two older ladies who had been good friends with his mom.

Then he made his way to a booth in the back of the

room. The waitress, Layne, followed. As he slid onto a seat, she rested one hip against the tabletop. He had gone to school with her and her brother, Cole, though he had been ahead of them both.

"You'd have thought you all knew I was coming," he said.

"We did." She grinned. "Sugar had a call from Jed. He said he had run into you at the hardware store."

And no doubt had hung around to listen in on his conversation with Ally.

He laughed, shaking his head. "I should have known. Things haven't changed much since I left for school." The older man probably had business to take care of in the store. It might even have required him to spend some time in the next aisle over from where they had met. Either way, it wouldn't have mattered. He knew Jed had been friends with his parents since long before he'd been born. And there was no denying the man always kept an ear to the ground about anything that went on in town.

"No, things don't change much here," Layne agreed. "Except for getting married and having kids, most of us are living the same lives as when we graduated from Cowboy Creek High. Not like yours."

If she only knew. And she would know soon enough.

The whole town would hear about it when he brought his brand-new son to the ranch. They all would learn he had been made a fool of by a woman who, as it turned out, was looking for a good time, not a husband. Not a baby—not even her own.

He would have Sean with him now, except when he had headed to Cowboy Creek yesterday morning, he didn't know what condition he would find the house in. He also didn't know whether he'd be able to find someone to watch the baby while he took care of putting things to rights.

On his arrival, he had discovered the house dusty but livable and, better luck, had solved part of that last concern. His quick trip to the hardware store for some basic supplies might have given him an answer to the other part.

"Speaking of babies—" Layne said.

He started, wondering if she'd read his thoughts.

"—my brother married Jed's granddaughter Tina—I don't know if you knew—and they just had their second baby. His other two granddaughter's are married now, too. And did you hear about Shay O'Neill?"

All three of the names she'd mentioned were familiar to him from school—inevitable in Cowboy Creek, as there was only one grade school, one junior high, one high school. "No, nobody mentioned Shay. What's up with her?"

"She's trying to outdo us all." Layne laughed. "She had triplets."

"Triplets?" He shook his head in wonder and thought about Sean. He couldn't begin to imagine taking care of more than one baby at a time.

Layne slipped her order pad from her uniform pocket. "What can I get you?"

"I'll wait. Ally Martinez is meeting me here. But you probably know that already, too."

She laughed in acknowledgment before walking away. Just as she disappeared through the doorway into the kitchen, the front door of the shop opened, and Ally entered.

Her long dark curls tumbled down almost to her

waist and bounced as she walked toward him. She had never been tiny, and she had filled out more in the years since he had last seen her. With her gleaming dark eyes, rosy cheeks and snug orange T-shirt, she gave the bright pink seats and decorations in the sandwich shop some competition. He recalled her hanging around the school-yard in grade school. He had been a couple of years ahead of her. Even that long ago, she had always acted larger than life—and been the life of the party.

Thinking of Sean, he frowned. Maybe Ally as a babysitter wouldn't be such a good influence on a pre-teen or a teenager...but a one-month-old? What could it hurt? Besides, even if she accepted the offer he planned to present to her, he and the baby wouldn't be here long enough for her to make much of an impact.

"Hi." Sounding a little breathless, she took the booth across from him. "I got here as soon as I could."

"Hope you didn't have to rush."

"No rush. No more than usual, anyhow. My papa says I never run at half speed when I can take it up to full." She laughed. "But I'm running behind now be-cause, just as I was leaving, one of the customers came to the register with a big order."

Since they had met up at the store, she had slicked something on her lips, shiny and red as cherry candy. Suddenly, he felt an urge to lean across the tabletop for a taste.

Whoa, Nelly.

He'd been away from women too long. Or not long enough.

Sex wasn't supposed to be on his radar for a good while into the future. Preferably, at least not till Sean turned twenty-one. He tried to think back to his school days and the younger Ally, when the few years' age difference between them seemed to be a much wider gap.

"Is something wrong?" she asked. "You're frowning."

"No. Nothing's wrong. I'm just trying to decide what to have. To drink."

Layne returned to the booth, and they each ordered sweet tea without the sweet and a wedge of lemon.

Ally sat fiddling with an armload of gold bracelets she wore on one wrist. She hadn't had them on at the store, he'd noticed…then wondered why he'd taken note of her bare, tanned arm in the first place. Anyhow, she probably didn't want the bracelets to get damaged while she was stocking shelves.

"We have the same taste in drinks," she said a moment later.

"I guess we do."

They made small talk until their teas arrived. Ally's quick drink left the straw candy-tipped from her lipstick. She smiled at him. "So, how has the big, bad city been treating you all these years? Well enough, I guess, or you would have been home again before now."

"Houston did treat me well, I have to admit." The woman he had met just before graduation was another story. "Going to school there was a good experience, one I don't regret. But I'm not in Houston anymore. I've got a job outside San Antonio, sales manager for a distributor of farming equipment."

She blinked those big dark eyes. "Why would you be selling farm equipment, when you have a ranch right here to come home to?"

"It pays the bills."

"Oh." His curt reply had thrown her. It didn't keep

her down for long. "Well, I can certainly see the benefits of that."

He hoped so. Just as he hoped this meeting would benefit them both. But he wanted to lead up to his idea slowly. And he didn't want to say too much about the past. If he had his way, neither Ally nor anyone else in Cowboy Creek would learn what happened between him and the woman he'd loved and had thought loved him, too.

He grabbed his tea glass. He had skipped the straw and now took such a long swallow, ice cubes clattered against his front teeth. "What about you? You didn't sound so overjoyed about the job at the store."

Even with her tanned skin and the pink makeup on her cheeks, he saw the telltale darkening of her flush. "I was just joking, pointing out the differences between us. Actually, it's a great job. Of course, I could always use some extra money. Who couldn't? But there's not a lot of work in Cowboy Creek, unless you're a cowboy or want to help decorate for weddings at the Hitching Post. I'd rather decorate a cowboy."

She shot him a flirty grin. "Kidding again, in case you didn't catch that. But, honestly, since I still live at home, my bills aren't too bad."

"How are your parents doing?"

"Great. Papa's still working at the car dealership, and Mama's still spoiling us both, making us breakfast before we head out to work every morning." She laughed. "Mama's always complaining my hours cut into *her* beauty sleep. But I'm an early riser, which means the seven-to-three shift works for me. Plus, it leaves my evenings free."

The perfect opening. "Yeah, so you'd said. You still like to hang out at the Cantina?"

"Sometimes. My friends and I will go there for the dance nights. Or go to the movies or bowling. You know, all the highlights of Cowboy Creek."

He laughed. "Yeah. I remember. I wanted to ask about the time you said you had free. While I'm here, I could use some help in the late afternoon and maybe some evenings."

Ally reached for her tea glass again and hoped Reagan couldn't see her hand shaking. This was Reagan Chase, the boy she had had a crush on all through school, the boy who had barely seemed to notice she was alive. Even back then, to her, he had looked hotter than a jalapeño— and he had grown up to become a man who looked ten times better than he had years ago.

And that man wanted her help.

"Of course," she said brightly, trying to hide her elation. "I'd be happy to give you a hand. Since you haven't been home since…since your mama and then your father died, I'm sure there's a lot to be done at the house. I'm sorry about your parents, Reagan," she said in a softer tone, "and sorry I never had the chance to tell you before today."

How could she—or anyone else in Cowboy Creek— have told him? He hadn't been home since before his mama died.

He nodded.

She hesitated, then said, "It's been over a year since your father passed. What brings you home now?"

He looked down at his glass. She felt sure he wouldn't answer. Too late, she realized maybe she shouldn't have asked.

Finally, he said, "The right way to phrase that question probably is why haven't I come back before now." He shrugged. "This was the first chance I had to get here."

"Well, I'm glad you're back. Everyone else will be, too. And I'm happy to help you empty closets, sort through cabinets, do some cleaning."

But not clearing out. Now you're here, tell me you're going to stay.

"Thanks," he said, "but that's not the kind of help I need."

Because you are planning to stay.

Her heart nearly jumped from joy. She couldn't help the reaction. She'd had years of history behind her when it came to caring about Reagan.

"That's fine, too," she assured him. "If it's anything to do with paperwork, I can help. I do some of the parts orders and the filing at the store. And Tina's a book-keeper. She'll help me out if you need to do anything with financial paperwork or taxes. So…what can I do for you?"

He smiled, and her heart gave an extra thump.

"While I'm in town," he said, "I need a babysitter."

Chapter Two

Reagan's matter-of-fact statement sent a shock wave all the way down to Ally's toes. "A…" She gulped. "A b-babysitter?"

"Yes."

"For a baby? *Your* baby?" Now, her heart plummeted. He had a child. Did he also have a wife?

Why hadn't she thought of that before she had agreed to meet him here? Wildly, she sent her gaze to his hand then back to his clear blue eyes. No ring on his finger. Not that a lack of one meant much. She saw enough married men, especially cowboys and ranchers, come into the store without their wedding rings. Jewelry could become a hazard to people who worked around equipment and livestock.

If *she* were married, she would wear a ring. She would want people to see the symbol of her love, of her devotion—once it was a done deal. However, she hadn't met the right cowboy yet…because no other cowboy could live up to Reagan Chase.

"Yes," he said, "I need a babysitter for my baby. I'm not married," he added flatly.

Relief flooded through her. Though curiosity about

his past filled her, too, she knew she had to focus on the here and now. She nodded, not sure what to say.

"It's a long story. One I'd rather not get into. But I have a one-month-old son. I've got someone to watch him during the day. You know Mrs. Browley?"

"Of course. She's one of my mama's best friends."

"She was to my mom, too. They spent a lot of time together at the women's club and planning events at the community center."

"I remember," she said softly. "Everyone misses her."

"Yeah." He stripped the covering from the straw he hadn't used and concentrated on wrapping it around his fingers. "Anyway, I stopped by Mrs. B's place to talk with her on my way here to Sugar's. She said she'll watch my son during the mornings and early afternoons. I'll be back again from San Antonio two days from now, and I already made arrangements to drop him off directly there. Then I expect to be busy out at the ranch all day." He took another long swallow of his tea.

As he tipped his head back to drink, she watched the muscles working in his throat. When he set the glass down, a rim of tea still wet his upper lip. He licked the moisture away. She shivered and glanced down at the tabletop.

"I'll call you to confirm I'm back," he said. "If you could pick him up at her house once you get off work in the afternoons, it would be a big help. I'm bound to be filthy from prowling around the ranch, and I'd lose a lot of good work time if I had to stop and shower up to come into town in the middle of the day."

At the thought of him in the shower, she shivered again. Trying to blame her reactions on her iced drink, she tightened her hand around the tall glass.

"I'll pay you whatever it is you make hourly at the store," he told her.

I don't want your money.

But how could she say that? He would find it highly suspicious, especially since she had said she could use the extra cash. And she couldn't confess to him that minding his baby scared the heck out of her. Not meeting his eyes, she sipped her tea and then touched the paper napkin to her lips.

She thought of all the years she had crushed on Reagan. Everyone in school probably knew how she felt about him. He must have known it, too. He couldn't have missed it…could he? Now the idea made her cringe. If he had noticed, she couldn't risk saying something that would make him recall how much she had liked him…and maybe make him change his mind about asking for her help.

Worse, if she didn't guard her reactions now, he would find out how much she still cared.

"You'd…want me to take the baby home with me until you pick him up?" That would work. Mama could help her with him.

"He'll be fine with Mrs. B all day, I know that. But his routine will already be upset enough since he won't be with his regular sitter. I'd rather you bring him out to the ranch and watch him there, if that's not a problem for you."

She was stuck between a rock and a hard place, as Jed Garland would say. She would go out to Reagan's family home to spend afternoons and evenings with him…and a baby she had no idea how to handle.

Fear at her inexperience fought with her longing to be with Reagan.

His small smile crinkled the corners of his eyes. His expression looked hopeful…and just a bit desperate.

Longing left her light-headed. Reagan needed her.

This was the chance she had always wanted to get close to him.

Well, if she could play the role of The Girl Most Likely to Make You Laugh, she could also convince herself she would be an expert babysitter. "No worries," she said firmly. "Watching the baby out at the ranch won't be a problem at all."

"BUT, TINA," ALLY WAILED, "what was I thinking? I don't know anything about babies!"

After her meeting with Reagan at SugarPie's, she had come out to the Hitching Post to see Tina, as she had told Jed she would.

Her best friend reclined on the couch in her newly renovated attic apartment at her family's hotel. She cuddled her sleeping newborn daughter close to her and laughed softly. "I know exactly what you were thinking. This is Reagan you're talking about."

Ally's cheeks flamed. From the time she and Tina had become best friends, they had shared all their secrets, including her crush on Reagan.

"And, *of course*, you know something about babies," Tina went on. "You held Emilia yesterday."

"Held. For a few seconds. That's a lot different from watching one for an entire afternoon and evening. Maybe for an entire week of afternoons and evenings." If she were lucky. Or possibly unlucky.

She didn't know what to hope for anymore. She ran her hands through her hair. Curls bounced in all directions, nearly blocking her vision. She swept them aside.

Tina laughed again. "That's my Ally, always the drama queen."

"You know it." She flounced into the upholstered chair near the couch. Even with her best friend, she sometimes felt the need to pretend. One of these days, The Girl Most Likely to Make You Laugh might have to fess up.

"You've also been around from the day Robbie was born." Robbie was Tina and her husband Cole's five-year-old.

"Okay, so I've played toy horses with him, and racing cars and once—a long time ago—I rolled a ball to him when he was still too little to move out of the way. He couldn't miss it," she admitted to Tina. "But I never fed him. Or gave him a bottle. Or—" she shuddered "—changed his diapers."

Shuddering aside, it wasn't diapers that bothered her so much as her fear Reagan's son would react to her the way other babies had. "Little kids and I just don't get along. The minute they see me, they know they're dealing with an amateur, and they all turn into howling, stiff-limbed little monsters."

Why had she ever thought she could take care of Reagan's baby?

"Ally, that's just silly. Come here." Tina sat upright on the couch.

Reluctantly, Ally crossed to take a seat beside her and let her place the newborn into her arms. The blanket-wrapped baby felt warmer and heavier than Ally had expected. Ally smiled down at her.

"See? Not so bad, is it?"

"You've got such a treasure here, *mi amiga*," she told Tina in a murmur, afraid her voice might startle the child. Better to let her sleep. Her goddaughter had an angelic face with a tiny cupid's-bow mouth, both of which Ally worried might be deceiving.

"Andi and I can teach you all you need to know." Tina's cousin had two small children of her own.

"Oh, right. An entire Baby 101 course, compressed into a couple of days?"

"Sure. You're a quick study. Piece of cake."

"Don't mention cake," she said with a moan. The baby moved her arm slightly, and Ally lowered her voice again. "I could eat an entire pan of your *abuela's* sopaipilla cheesecake right this minute."

Tina smiled. "I don't think it's on the menu tonight. But stay for supper. By the time we're done, Emilia will need another feeding and a diaper change, and we'll get you started on some hands-on experience."

"This might be all the hands-on I can handle. But I suppose I can stay." Truthfully, the deciding factor was more the thought of Tina's grandmother's cooking than it was the lessons.

"What I want to know," she said thoughtfully, "is exactly where Reagan's baby came from."

"Uh...Ally? We covered the birds and the bees in about fifth grade."

She rolled her eyes. "Not fair, *chica*. As I always tell you, you're supposed to be the serious half of this friendship. I get all the funny lines."

"Unfortunately, I don't see anything funny about this situation."

That made her look at Tina in alarm. Her friend always *was* the serious one. If she were worried, chances were good there was something to be concerned about. "What?"

"Well…" Tina shrugged. "You have a point. Forgetting about the birds and bees, the question still stands. Where did Reagan's baby come from?"

"I don't know. He didn't want to talk about it."

"That sounds ominous."

"You mean there has to be a wife somewhere? But he said he wasn't married." Her voice had risen, and Emilia shifted in her arms again. "Here. I think she's waking up. You'd better take her before she opens her eyes, sees me and starts to yell."

Tina shook her head at Ally but reached for her daughter. "Then maybe Reagan has an ex-wife. Or a girlfriend, either ex or current. Or he could be widowed."

She gasped. "With a one-month-old baby?" They exchanged suddenly misty-eyed glances. "Oh, I hope not. It would be best if he had gotten a di—" She stopped.

"Divorce," Tina supplied in a soft voice, "because then Reagan wouldn't be attached to another woman."

"Well…" She glanced down at her hands in her lap. Then, sighing, she looked at Tina again. "Yes," she admitted finally. Feeling miserable, she yanked on one of her curls. How could she wish away a poor defenseless little baby's mother?

Yet how could she *not* want a chance at winning the boy she had always loved?

WITH THE HITCHING POST'S guests all gone up to their rooms for the night, Jed Garland went along the hall of the first-floor family wing. He wandered into the hotel's kitchen, where Paz, the hotel cook, stood at the counter making preparations for next morning's breakfast. Tina, the granddaughter he and Paz had in common, sat at the big table with her new baby in her arms.

He settled in his chair across from the pair of them. "You're starting that little one off with late hours, are you?"

She laughed. "She's the one setting her own schedule, *Abuelo*. This baby likes to eat and sleep as she pleases. I just follow along to do her bidding."

"Well, that's the way it should be when they're that young." He kicked back and laced his fingers together on the tabletop. "I see Ally's finally showing some maternal instincts." The girl had come out to the hotel and stayed for supper, then spent the evening in the sitting room with his granddaughters and their kids.

"I don't know about maternal instincts," she said doubtfully. "Ally always claims she and babies don't get along. And of course she won't admit she remembers all the time she's spent with Robbie, including when he was an infant. Anyhow, Andi and I need to give her a crash course in infant care. She's going to be babysitting Reagan's little boy."

"So *that's* why Reagan wanted to talk with her at Sugar's."

"You heard about that already?" She shook her head. "There's no doubt about it, is there? News really does travel fast in Cowboy Creek."

"I happened to be at the hardware store when Ally and Reagan ran into each other."

"Oh, is that so?" She stared him down. He looked back at her, keeping his gaze level. "Funny. I thought Ally said Reagan invited her at the end of their conversation, after you had left."

"He did. It so happens I had to pick up some supplies in the next aisle, and I overheard what they were saying."

Both women laughed at that, as he had known they would.

"I'll bet you did," Tina said. "I'll also bet Sugar called you right after they left the shop, didn't she?"

Now it was his turn to laugh. His youngest granddaughter usually had the knack of seeing right through him. "You won't let me get away with anything, will you? Yes, Sugar did call. So, Reagan has a child. And a wife?"

"Ally said he told her no on that."

"Good." He beamed.

Tina's eyes narrowed. "Why? You're scheming again, aren't you?"

"Do you blame me?"

She shot a quick smile at her grandmother, then reached across the table and squeezed Jed's laced fingers. "You wouldn't be you, *Abuelo*, if you didn't care so much about everyone. This is between you, me and *Abuela* only, but…Ally has always had a crush on Reagan."

"Well, then, all the more reason for me to get up to some scheming, as you called it. Surely, you can't object if I want to help her."

Now she looked down and touched her baby's cheek. "No, I can't say I really object. Ally's my best friend. I want her to be as happy as I am."

"Good. First, we'll have to find out exactly what Reagan's status is. If he's unattached…"

"Any free man is fair game?"

"Exactly right."

"Ally would never speak to me again if she knew I was encouraging you to play matchmaker for her."

"And that's exactly right, too," he said with a grin. "*If she knew.* But there's no need for her or Reagan to find out."

"And how will you manage that, Jed?" Paz asked. She dried her hands on a towel and took a seat at the table. The fine silver threads in her dark hair winked in the overhead light.

"I haven't quite figured that out yet. But don't you worry, I'm ready and willing to face the challenge. I'll come up with something."

"You won't have much time," Tina told him. "Ally said Reagan is leaving again as soon as he has the house cleared out and ready to go on the market."

"Then I'll have to work quickly, won't I?" He smiled. "Fortunately, as you both know, I do my best work under pressure."

ALLY TOOK A deep breath and climbed the porch to Mrs. Browley's front door. It sure wasn't the idea of seeing her mama's friend that made her need the reassurance. Taking another deep breath, she rang the doorbell and filled her mind with positive thoughts.

Piece of cake. Sopaipilla cheesecake. I can do this.

A few moments later, the door opened and she was greeted with a friendly welcome and a big hug. The older woman who stood beaming at her wore her white hair pulled back into her usual bun and eyed Ally over a pair of wire-rimmed glasses.

"Hi, Mrs. Browley. I'm here to pick up the special delivery package you're holding for me."

Mrs. Browley laughed. "Ally. Come in, dear. That

little package of yours is waiting happily to make your acquaintance."

That wouldn't last long.

Slowly, she followed the woman down the hallway to the kitchen. She glanced at the padded diaper bag sitting on the small table. She looked at the baby carrier resting beside it. And finally, she stared at the baby inside the carrier.

He was tiny, not much bigger than Tina's newborn. A few wispy curls lay against his scalp. "His hair's so much lighter than Reagan's," she blurted.

"It is," Mrs. Browley agreed. "That may darken as he gets older. Or he may take after his mother."

She shot a glance at the older woman. Could Reagan have told Mrs. Browley the "long story" he didn't want to share with her about why he wasn't married? But the other woman just looked down at the baby.

Ally did, too. The baby stared up at her, his eyes only half open.

"Those eyes, though," Mrs. Browley said, "are just like the blue of his daddy's. Aren't they, Sean?" The baby's eyelids drifted closed, then fluttered open. She laughed softly. "He just finished eating, and now he's fighting sleep. You should have a nice, quiet ride out to Reagan's ranch."

"I hope so." And with one feeding out of the way, she might get a reprieve from having to give the baby his bottle today. Two afternoons' worth of lessons with Tina and Andi had left her feeling a tiny bit more comfortable but nowhere near competent. And to her relief, at least neither Tina's infant nor Andi's little girl had protested when Ally held them. She had no guarantee of the same result with Reagan's baby.

Mrs. Browley gave a heavy sigh.

Ally tensed. "Is there something wrong?"

The other woman shook her head sadly. "Just thinking about yesterday. I saw Jed Garland at Sugar's, and we were discussing Reagan."

"You were?" Ally eyed her from under her lashes. This didn't sound promising. Everyone in town knew anytime Jed or Sugar involved a third party in one of their conversations, at least two of those three were up to something.

"We all knew both Reagan's parents, of course," Mrs. Browley said. "And we think that boy is going to have a hard time out at the ranch. Sandra was a wonderful wife and mother, and an excellent housekeeper, too. But she liked her crafts just as much as any of us in the women's circle do. And she was a fabulous cook. Their place was filled with so many of her handmade decorations, and lots of material and yarn and cookbooks and all kinds of kitchen equipment."

Ally tried not to grimace. At home, Mama often rolled her eyes and moaned that Ally would never learn to cook. She would reply she *did* know how— she did just fine with a box and a microwave, didn't she? "Wouldn't his father have gotten rid of some of those things, or given them away?"

"No. It was hard on Larry when Sandra got so sick. I know for a fact he couldn't bring himself to touch any of her things once she passed on." She rested her hand on Ally's arm. "Having your help with the baby will give Reagan more time to focus on what needs to be done."

And give her more time to waver between wanting to run from the ranch and longing to be with him.

"Well." She looked at the baby, whose eyes were

now fully closed. "I guess it's time to get moving with Sleepy Beauty here."

"*Sleeping Beauty*, I think you mean, dear. Although *she* was a girl, not a boy." Mrs. Browley's eyebrows dipped in a concerned frown.

"Don't worry." She laughed. "I do know the difference. You know I always joke when I'm feeling uptight."

"I wouldn't have thought that applied here. There's nothing to be nervous about. This little angel won't give you a bit of worry."

Ally nodded. She only wished she could feel as confident.

Chapter Three

No wonder Reagan didn't want to make the trip into town and back again twice in one day.

Ally had visited his family's ranch once and knew it was small compared with most of the properties around Cowboy Creek. The narrow rectangular piece of land lay tucked between two larger spreads. But the ride had been longer than she remembered.

As she pulled the car up to the ranch house, she peeked into her rearview mirror at the car seat Reagan had left for her at Mrs. Browley's house. Luckily, she had gotten instructions from Tina on the right way to install the seat in the car and then how to fasten the baby safely inside.

Another mirror suction-cupped to the back window reflected the infant's image. In the frequent quick peeks she had taken on the drive to the ranch, she hadn't seen him stir. Now, his eyes were open, blinking in the light, staring up at the mirror.

"Hey, baby," she said softly. "So, you're awake. Listen, the two of us are going to get along great. No tricks, no temper tantrums on your part. And only first-class care on mine. I promise you that. After all, I've been trained by the best. There's nothing like learning your trade from a brand-new mama."

She winced. As far as she knew, the baby didn't have a mama. Had he ever heard the word before? How would he react at hearing it from her?

But he lay still in his seat, blinking lazily.

She took a deep breath and let it out again. Now or never. She would rather never, but that hadn't been the agreement she had made with Reagan.

She went to the rear passenger door and knelt on the backseat to unhook the safety harness. "This is only your first time out here at the ranch, isn't it?" Her hands shook just a tiny bit. So did her voice.

The baby looked up at her. He had slept through the entire ride, as if the bouncing of her car on the frequently uneven road had soothed him. Maybe the wobbly sound of her voice had the same effect. If that was the case, she would let her nerves take over and talk to him all day long.

She transferred him to his baby seat and strapped him in. "I've only been out to the ranch once before. My mama and the other ladies of the women's circle sometimes have special Saturday meetings. And one Saturday a long time ago, when Mrs. Chase, your *abuela*—your grandma—had the meeting here, she invited all of the ladies to bring their kids along."

After hoisting her purse and the diaper bag onto one shoulder, she picked up the baby in his carrier.

So far, so good. Keep talking.

"This was when I was in junior high school. You'll find out all about school someday. Anyway, that Saturday, I got to see your daddy." The memory made her voice suddenly rise. She looked at the baby in alarm, but he simply stared up at her. "He was grooming his horse outside the barn. And would you believe, I got hit with an attack of shyness. Me, Ally Martinez, The Girl Most Likely to Make You Laugh. Crazy, isn't it? Well. I sat on the darned corral fence for almost an hour, never even saying hello, just watching him work."

As she went up the steps to the house, she shot a fond glance toward the corral. Then she looked down at the baby. Sean seemed transfixed by her story. Maybe there wouldn't be much to this babysitting, after all.

Reagan had told her the kitchen door at the back of the house would be open. She went inside and took the baby over to the table.

She hadn't gotten her fill of Reagan that day long ago, but it was the first time she had ever been able to sit and stare at him unnoticed by anyone. Including him, unfortunately.

"Your daddy's a couple of years older than I am," she explained. "Well…probably closer to three, and I guess he thought I was just a little kid. He never did pay much attention to me." Leaning closer to the baby, she whispered, "But let me tell you, things are going to change now. What do you think of that?"

The baby looked up and instantly gave her his answer. He stiffened his arms and legs, scrunched up his face and let out a screech.

"Hush," she said hurriedly, rocking the seat slightly. The movement did no good and even seemed to upset the baby more. "Shh-h-h. *Shh-h-h.* Don't cry, baby. Your daddy will hear you and fire me on the spot."

"I already hear him."

She jumped and let out a screech even louder than Sean's.

Reagan's voice had come from the other side of the kitchen. Reluctant to turn and face him, she stared down at the baby, whose face was getting redder by the minute. So was hers, judging by the heat flooding her cheeks. Reagan had heard the baby crying. But had he also heard anything she had said to the baby?

Suddenly, Reagan was standing beside her. He had sturdy hands with long fingers, and in seconds he had unfastened the straps around the baby. "When a kid's this wrought-up," he said, "rocking the seat's not going to help. He needs out of here." He lifted Sean and placed him against his shoulder.

She noted he cupped his hand around the back of the baby's head just the way Tina had taught her.

"Let me guess," he said. "Mrs. B fed him not long before you went to pick him up."

She nodded. "That's what she said. But he was fine in the car. He didn't let out a peep the entire trip."

"He's making up for it now." He patted the infant's back. "He's probably battling some gas from his formula."

Again, she nodded. In the past, she had heard both Tina and Andi say something similar about one of their babies. Obviously, it was common with little ones. Why hadn't she thought of that herself now?

She hadn't been in the house two minutes yet, and already she had given Reagan reason to think she couldn't handle the job he needed her to do.

SEAN SQUAWKED IN Reagan's ear. "Shh-h-h," he said, the way Ally had done. The baby quieted, but only a daddy with zero experience would expect that to last.

"Come on," he said, "while we can hear ourselves

talk, let me take you up and show you where to find all the baby's things." Leading the way, he left the kitchen and went to the stairs.

He was having trouble getting an image out of his mind, the sight of Ally leaning over the baby seat and whispering to his son. He had overheard the tail end of her one-sided conversation, and he was having trouble forgetting what she had said right before she had lowered her voice.

I guess he thought I was just a little kid. He never did pay much attention to me.

She meant him. And she was right. He *hadn't* paid her much mind years ago. Three years' difference, give or take, made a big gap between a grade-school girl and a kid in junior high. The division between junior high and high school had caused a greater divide. Then, it had seemed like a big reason to avoid her. Not that he'd had any interest in her, anyway. He *had* thought of her as just a kid.

But as he looked at her now—

Sean let out another squawk.

Good boy, trying to get his daddy's attention back where it belonged.

He cleared his throat and deliberately faced forward as they went along the upstairs hall. "Ignore the mess downstairs. When I was out here the other day, I got as far as cleaning the kitchen and bathroom, and that's it. You might've seen the baby's playpen in the corner of the kitchen."

"I did."

"I moved a portable television into that area, too, and a stack of magazines. You should avoid the other rooms downstairs until I have a chance to give them a good going-over. Upstairs, I've only tackled one bedroom and the bathroom. So this little guy and I are bunking together in my old room. The memories might remain, but at least the dust is gone."

A dumb statement. He hadn't meant it to come out sounding so pathetic. It was too late to take the words back and too late to stop Ally from following him into the room. He turned as she stopped short just inside the doorway and looked around.

He let his glance rove over what she was seeing. The baby's portable crib. The pine bedroom set. The shelves still filled with memorabilia from his childhood interests and high school days.

"Is this the way the room looked when you were a kid?" she asked. "With the football and baseball pennants and the autographed balls, the 4-H ribbons and all the trophies?"

"Yeah," he said sheepishly. "When I left for school, my mom wanted to leave everything the way it was. I think she believed I'd want to come back and relive the memories of all my school years."

"Those were the days," she said drily.

Was she thinking again about the times he hadn't paid attention to her?

Blinking, she gave him a small smile. "I'm sure she missed you a lot while you were gone."

"Yeah," he said gruffly. "You know…only child, and all that."

"Me, too. But unlike you, I never left my mama."

Again, he wished he could go back and change the past. If not for his fight with his dad, he might have gotten to see his parents a lot more in those years after he left for college. By the time he had earned his degree, he had lost any chance to see his mom at all. Then, a year ago, he had learned he'd never have the opportunity to mend fences with his dad.

He yanked a diaper from the sack in the top dresser drawer and laid a towel on the bed. It took him only a minute to show Ally where he had stored Sean's clothes and blankets.

While he changed the baby, she moved around the room, checking out the trophies. "Baseball," she said. "Football. Softball. Track. No wonder you were named all-around athlete the year you graduated."

When he glanced up, he found her looking at him. He turned his attention back to Sean. "You remember that?"

"I was there in the stadium the day they gave out the awards. Along with three-quarters of Cowboy Creek."

He remembered that day, too, and not because of the standing ovation.

"Is there any sport you don't play?" she asked.

"Not really," he said, grateful for the question and the chance to change the subject. "How about you? What's your favorite sport?"

"Telephone tag."

He laughed. She did, too, a low, sexy laugh very different from the high-pitched giggles he remembered hearing from her and her friends.

Sean let out another squawk.

"I guess he gets the joke, too," she said. "Smart baby."

"Yeah." Blinking, he focused again on his son.

An attraction to his boy's babysitter was something he hadn't expected. Something he sure didn't need, considering he planned to have her help him out as often as she could in the next week or two.

"I'd better get back to the job." Suddenly it seemed even more important to make progress. The sooner he finished up everything he needed to do here at the ranch, the better. "I spent most of this afternoon working in the barn and want to keep at it while the light's still good."

"That makes sense."

"Yeah." Luckily, she didn't comment on what would have made the most sense, tackling the house first so he could get it ready to sell. But if his bedroom held so many dusty memories, he hated to think what he would discover once he went through the rest of the rooms, the closets, the cubbyholes. "My dad has a lot stored out in the barn—tack and farm tools and all the other equipment you need to run a ranch."

"Like everything we sell at the store," she said. "He was a regular."

"Yeah. Of course you know all about farming and ranching equipment." She also probably knew more about both his parents' later years than he did.

He lifted Sean from the bed and rested him against his shoulder again.

She stood inspecting a couple of faded photographs tacked to a bulletin board above his student desk. He looked at the photos and couldn't help shaking his head. His mom had stuck them there just before graduation. Since he'd come home, he hadn't had the heart to take them down.

Ally turned and flashed him a brilliant smile. "Prom king. That was another pretty impressive announcement."

"Old times," he said shortly. "Things change."

"So I see." She gestured to the other photo, the one

he'd looked at more times in the past couple of days than he could count. "This is you and your parents when you were a kid, isn't it?"

"Yeah. One of my mom's favorite pictures, from a vacation we took to California."

"I guessed that from the big black mouse ears you're wearing. Maybe someday, you'll get Sean a pair of those."

"Maybe." Memories crowded his mind. Ally's light perfume stirred his senses. Suddenly feeling closed in, he said abruptly, "I'll show you where everything's at downstairs before I head back to the barn."

Then, until it was time for her to leave, he would stay there, working by the exposed overhead lights. Heck, by kerosene lamp, if he had to.

IN THE QUIET of Reagan's kitchen, it didn't take Ally long to grow bored.

While the baby slept in his crib, she kept the television volume turned low. She watched more than she wanted to of late-afternoon comedies and early-evening news. The television stations were beginning their prime-time shows before she realized how late it was. At the same time, Sean woke up.

She moved him into his carrier on the kitchen table.

"I'm getting pretty good at these straps and buckles, aren't I, baby?"

He looked up, his mouth pursed tightly, as if he were giving serious thought to what she had said.

"Oh, everybody's a critic," she told him. "I'm not expecting anything less from you than two thumbs-up."

A peek through the window over the sink showed her the light streaming through the open doors of the barn. She turned to the baby again. "Your daddy's still out there, and you know what? I don't believe he's ever coming back inside."

It was her turn to purse her lips for a moment. "He wasn't happy about those pictures in his bedroom, was he? Or maybe he wasn't happy about the fact that I saw them. I guess I can't argue about that. It has to be so hard for him, losing both his mama and daddy. Like you…" She peered down at the baby and asked softly, "Where's your mama, little one?"

Naturally, he didn't reply.

"Well, maybe you'll tell me someday." She smiled. "Your daddy said he's an only child, like me. But he has *you*, and that's a very good thing. I'll bet he misses you, too, while he's in the barn working all by himself. Let's go see." She picked up the carrier.

Outside, the night was still warm from the day's heat. It wasn't pitch-dark yet, but the moon already cast a faint glow against the dimness of the sky. "There's a man in that moon up there," she told Sean, "and one day, your daddy will show him to you."

As they approached the barn, she heard a noise she recognized from the store, the familiar sound of wooden planks thudding against one another. Through the doorway, she could see Reagan piling lumber in one corner near the stalls. He was so intent on his work, he didn't hear her enter, not even when she cleared her throat to get his attention.

Oh, well. She had done what she could, hadn't she? It wouldn't be fair to call out his name and startle him.

Instead, she stood there getting a good look. She took in the sight of his threadbare jeans, his sweat-dampened back, his muscles bunching and flexing as he shifted one load after another of scrap lumber.

It wasn't until she stood admiring his pecs and abs that she realized he had turned and stood looking at her.

Oops.

Recovering quickly, she gave a wolf whistle. "You need to apply for a job at the store. Think what having you on the payroll will do for our profits. After one look at you, all the women in Cowboy Creek will instantly become do-it-yourselfers."

"I don't think so."

"Oh, but I *do*. Keep in mind I'm comfortable making the suggestion because I get paid by the hour. You wouldn't have to worry about cutting into my commissions."

"With all the wranglers who must stop in just to see you, I'd probably have to worry more about you cutting into mine."

"A *compliment*, Reagan Chase?" she said archly, batting her lashes like one of the actresses from her mama's favorite late-night movies. "How unexpected. But I'm flattered."

He looked as if he had had second thoughts about what he had said. Maybe she'd overdone it on the exaggerated flirting attempt.

"Yeah. Well." His smile seemed forced. "Don't let it go to your head."

"Oh, I won't." No chance of that. His words had gone straight to her heart. Obviously, she had been foolish to think he had meant them.

Afraid he might read the truth behind her teasing, she looked down at the baby for just a moment. "Sean and I were wondering if you were planning to eat tonight."

"Eat?" His gaze went to the open doorway behind her. "What time is it?"

"Sevenish."

"Dang." He ran his hand through his hair, giving her another look at flexing muscle. "I lost track of time. And I showed you the baby's formula, but I didn't tell you what food I'd stocked in the kitchen for grownups, did I?"

"No."

"Sorry. I stopped at the L-G this morning after I dropped Sean at Mrs. B's." The Local-General Store in the heart of town served most of Cowboy Creek. "I didn't pick up a full order yet, but there're sandwich fixings in the refrigerator and a loaf of bread in the box near the toaster. Help yourself."

"You're not planning to eat?"

His gaze sliding away from her, he shook his head. "I've still got a lot to do out here."

"Won't you wear yourself out if you don't pace yourself?"

"Who, me? I'm an all-around athlete, remember?"

"I'll never forget." She had attempted her arch tone again, but the words rang embarrassingly true, at least to her.

Judging by Reagan's suddenly blank stare, he noticed her mistake, too.

As she had told Sean, his daddy either didn't want to resurrect memories or didn't like the idea of sharing them with her. A shame, really.

She shifted the baby carrier on her arm, making an effort to remember she wasn't here for fun and games, reminding herself Reagan wasn't interested in flirting.

An even bigger shame, because that was what she

did best. She didn't intend to give it up at this crucial point—though, of course, she'd cut back on the fake vampiness from now on.

Experience had taught her flirting was guaranteed to get a man's attention. And she definitely wanted to capture Reagan's.

Chapter Four

As he finished piling the lumber into stacks off to one side of the barn, Reagan shook his head at himself. His plan to stay out of the house until it was time for Ally to leave for home hadn't been very well thought out. And it hadn't been very bright.

With plenty of work and then some to keep him busy, he could have kept going for hours. But he could hardly hang out in the barn all night. His son had to be changed and settled into his portable crib upstairs. He didn't expect Ally to handle that. In fact, he hadn't expected her to stay this late. If not for him, she wouldn't have.

He knew it was too little effort, too late, but he made his way quickly toward the house.

Clouds covered the moon, and he had only the back porch light that Ally must have put on, plus the square of light from the kitchen window, to guide his footsteps through the dark. It reminded him of all the nights when he was growing up and had come in from working in the barn or, as he got older, out on the land with his dad. In the earliest days, they were two tough ranchers—one of them still in diapers and short pants.

At the sudden memories of later days, his stomach knotted.

When he entered the kitchen, Ally looked up. She sat near the darkened television in the corner, thumbing through one of the outdated magazines he had left in a pile on the counter. She had tuned his mom's old radio to a station now playing music with a fast beat, but she had left the sound turned low.

The baby lay sleeping in the playpen.

"So you finally decided to quit for the night," she said.

"Yeah." He glanced across the room and noted the napkin-covered plate sitting on one side of the table. "You didn't eat yet?"

"I did, since I had no idea what time you'd be coming in. I made an extra sandwich in case you walked in feeling ravenous." She gave him a bright smile.

Suddenly, he did have a huge appetite, but not one connected to food.

"I'm good, thanks." He looked away, checking in on the baby again from a distance. "I'm too covered in dirt to go near Sean, but I can see he's sleeping soundly."

"He hasn't moved for a long time," she confirmed.

"Good. He's usually tucked in bed by now." *Great.* He'd as good as told her he had stayed outside long past the time he'd normally have taken care of his son. "Since this is your first day with the baby, I'll give you both a break. You can skip the bedtime routine with him this time."

"Okay." She began straightening the stack of magazines.

He shucked his boots and left them near the outside door. While he was still out in the barn, he had thought briefly of the no-frills shower stall off in one corner. But he'd only scrubbed his hands at the sink. It didn't make sense to clean up out there, as his clothes were filthy and he'd be carrying dirt from them into the house, anyhow.

If Ally hadn't been there, he could have left his jeans and T-shirt outside on the porch. He envisioned stripping off his clothes in front of her. "I need a cold shower," he said abruptly.

For a moment, she looked as rattled as he felt. Her glance went from his socks to his jeans to his sweaty T-shirt, where it lingered a moment before finally rising to his face. Here he was having hot thoughts about her, and she seemed worried about dirt in the house. If so, she'd best not hope to become a rancher's wife.

"Sean will sleep for a while now," he told her. "I'll let him carry on while I go get cleaned up. I can take over from here. We didn't discuss how you want to be paid. Daily or at the end of the week?"

Again, she looked upset. He frowned. "Did I forget to say I'd want the help for at least a week, if not two?"

"You mentioned it when we talked at SugarPie's. You weren't very specific."

"That's because I'm not sure. It depends on how long it takes me to get the house in shape." A heckuva long time if he didn't do more than what he'd done already, which meant clean the minimum of rooms so he and Sean could stay here comfortably. And temporarily. "If you expect to run into a problem, let me know now. I'll talk to Mrs. B and maybe Sugar, have them start spreading the word to see if I can find someone else."

"No," she blurted.

Obviously, her distress about the dirt on his clothes was nothing compared with the thought of losing her short-term job. She must need the extra money more than she had let on.

"It's fine," she said. "I won't have any trouble working for you for a couple of weeks or…or even longer. I told you, once I'm done at the store, my time is my own. And speaking of stores, you weren't kidding when you said you didn't pick up much at the L-G. If you want to give me a list, I could swing by there tomorrow before I get the baby at Mrs. Browley's."

"You're here for Sean. I don't expect you to do the shopping."

"The store is on my route. And you said yourself it's a big hassle to stop working to run into town."

He hesitated, then nodded. "It is. And I drop Sean off at Mrs. B's before the L-G's open. It would be a help if you'd grab a few things for me on your way out here. I could be that much closer to getting done, and you could make some extra money for your time."

Judging by her fallen expression, that comment didn't go over well with her, either. Funny. He'd thought for sure she would have been happy about the additional pay.

Women. He'd never figure them out.

But then, considering he and Sean had been deserted by one, hadn't he realized that already?

"I'M SURPRISED YOU'RE HERE," Tina said to Ally as they settled into the comfy overstuffed chairs in the Hitching Post's sitting room. "You told me Reagan has you bringing the baby out to his place after work."

"We're on the way. But trust me, Reagan won't notice what time we get there."

Yesterday, when she had arrived at the ranch with Sean and the groceries, Reagan had been nowhere to be found. She had given up on the television altogether and spent the hours with the radio and the stack of magazines again. She was already bored and lonely with no one to talk to but a sleeping baby. By the time Reagan came into the house, she had begun wishing she had stopped by the Hitching Post to occupy her time.

And Reagan certainly didn't hang around to chat.

Once he'd taken off his boots, checked on the baby and said good-night to her, he disappeared even more quickly than he had the night before.

Outside, she had stood for a moment beside her car, looking up at the light in the second-floor window and longing to be a fly on the wall in his shower—or at least to have the pleasure of seeing his silhouette in the window. Then, blushing at her own thoughts, she had gotten into the car and driven away.

Her gaze hadn't strayed to the rearview mirror more than a half-dozen times.

"Well," Tina said, "I'm glad you made the detour here. We're so glad to see you—*both* of you."

"You don't need to sound so excited about it," Ally told her. "Does she?" she asked the baby as she took off the light blanket she had used to shield him from the midafternoon sun.

"Why not?" Tina asked. "Sean doesn't look traumatized by having you near him, the way you said all babies do. Aren't things going well with Reagan?"

"That's your daddy," Ally explained to the child. Somehow it seemed easier to admit the truth aloud to him than to her own best friend. That's what frustration did to you. Or maybe humiliation. "You know your daddy, right? So do I. But he doesn't seem to have a clue who I am."

"Have I missed something?" Tina's cousin Andi entered the room holding her daughter, who, Ally thought, was just over a year old.

With all the kids around the Hitching Post and all the newborns in town, it was hard to keep track. Only a few months ago, one of their friends from school had even had a set of triplets. Ally gave thanks Reagan had come to town with a single infant. As cooperative as Sean had been so far, one baby at a time was still more than enough for her.

"I don't know," Tina said to her cousin. "I've been here for the entire conversation, but I'm not sure what we're talking about, either."

Andi laughed and set her daughter into the playpen in the corner.

Jed Garland had helped match up quite a few couples over the past year or two, including all three of his granddaughters. Andi, the middle one, was a slim, gorgeous blonde. This should have put three strikes against her in Ally's book except the woman was so darned *nice*. And after all the sadness she had faced in her life not long ago, Ally was glad she had found new love with an old flame—which is what they would call Andi's romance in one of her mama's daytime television shows. And which was exactly what Ally was trying to do with Reagan.

Unfortunately, carrying a torch—as Mama would put it—had gotten her nowhere due to lack of encouragement on his part. But why would he do anything to give her hope? He wasn't carrying a torch for her. And he never had.

Andi smiled. "It looks like our lessons are paying off. You seem very comfortable around the baby."

"It's hard not to be. He never gives me any trouble."

She shrugged. "Of course, he might just be sizing up the situation. I've only been minding him for two days now." The time seemed to have gone by so quickly when she thought about taking care of the baby, yet so slowly in terms of her progress with Reagan. "Sean just eats and sleeps, and that's about it."

"That's what they do at this age," Tina said, looking down at her daughter.

"It means he's comfortable with you, too," Andi said. "In fact, he's probably getting attached."

"Well, I wish some of that comfort and attachment would come from the direction of his daddy."

There, she'd said it. And in front of Andi, too. Did she have no shame? But why try to hide how she felt about Reagan now? After the afternoons of Baby 101, her feelings had to have become obvious to Andi—but she surely hoped not to anyone else at the Hitching Post.

She shook her head. "Reagan's avoiding me, I think, doing anything he can to stay out of my way. He only comes into the house at the end of the night, right before I leave, to..."

To go upstairs to strip off his jeans and T-shirt.

Every day at the hardware store—and almost every day of her life—she saw plenty of men in clothes just like Reagan's. But worn-out and filthy or not, *his* clothes had somehow become the sexiest she'd ever seen on a man.

"Um...hello? Ally?" Tina said. "You've got us holding our breath here. Reagan comes into the house to..."

Startled, she blushed. "Sorry. I was...uh...thinking about Sean's next bottle. Anyway, Reagan comes in for the night, checks for updates on how the baby is doing and that's it. I'm dismissed."

"He puts in a long day working. He's probably tired." Though Andi's expression and tone were serious, her comments left Ally laughing.

They also helped her revert to the girl everyone knew best. "Yes, he's tired. He's exhausted from having me look at him like he's tastier than Paz's sopaipilla cheesecake."

"Wow," Andi said. "That's a seriously delicious example. If that's what you compare him to, you must have it bad."

"Awful," she agreed. She looked down at Sean and wiggled his foot. "I shouldn't even admit this in front of the baby."

"Admit what?" Tina asked.

"His daddy can pretend all he likes that I don't exist—outside of being his babysitter, that is." She smiled slowly. "But somehow, I'm going to make the man see I can be much more than that."

ONLY FRIDAY, AND it had seemed like the longest week of his life.

Reagan had spent his days riding the small ranch, checking the fence line and boundaries, looking for signs of any predators or other problems. If there was anything that might make a prospective buyer hesitate, he wanted to head that off at the pass.

He'd spent his evenings in the barn. But even for a man working solo, there was only so much to be done. With no livestock in the stalls, no feed in the bins, no tack or equipment being used on a regular basis, he'd run out of things to sort through and maintain. Run out of reasons to avoid Ally.

Reluctantly, he turned his steps to the house. He

could see the usual back porch and kitchen lights shining, almost calling out to him. He wouldn't mind an early night for once, a chance to spend time with his son before the baby went to bed. Back home, he'd had more time with Sean than this. But *this* couldn't last much longer. Or neither would he.

All week long, he had fought second thoughts about asking Ally to help him out.

Sometime during those days, he had begun thinking about *asking* Ally out.

And that was crazy.

Inside the house, he followed the sound of her favorite salsa music to the living room. He found her with a dust cloth in her hand and her back to him, dancing in front of the bookshelves set along the far wall. She had tied a bright red bandanna around her nearly black hair. Big gold hoop earrings, normally half hidden by her curls, dangled close to her cheeks.

Sean looked up at him from his baby seat, which had been set on a dust-free and polished end table placed just inside the doorway. The table sat well away from both the radio and the rapidly moving cloth.

Reagan crossed the room and punched the button on the radio. The music abruptly stilled. So did Ally. Then she turned to face him, her face flushed from the exertion of her dancing.

"You're in early," she said, her voice rising to a squeak.

"Yeah." He gestured toward the cloth. "What are you doing?"

"Dusting."

He grinned. "I can see that. Were you angling for double time?"

"No," she snapped. Not a squeak within earshot now.

Her dark eyes flashed. "I was just trying to help you because…" Her cheeks turned even pinker.

"Because?"

"Because I want to. I don't like what's on TV right now, and the magazines had started to bore me. You haven't had any time to start working in the house—"

He hadn't *made* any time.

"—so I thought I'd give you a hand in here. There might be some things my mama thinks I'll never learn to do, but she made sure dusting a room isn't one of them."

He raised his brows. "Is that so?"

Now, she flushed beet red and refused to look his way. She ran the cloth over a couple of the bookshelves, bending down to reach the lower ones, giving him a substantial, satisfying view he'd bet she didn't intend for him to see. He had no idea how good a job she did as a house cleaner. But she sure knew how to fill out every inch of denim in a pair of jeans.

He tried not to think about the sudden tightness in his own jeans.

Okay, his increasing interest in her all this week was perfectly normal and to be expected. He was a red-blooded male, wasn't he? And one who hadn't been to bed with a woman in over nine months.

But Ally was a whole different story.

Years ago, thanks to his success in sports, he had developed a fan club of kids from school. He'd gotten used to seeing the younger girl in that crowd but never realized she felt a special liking for him. Now, he was mature enough to see it.

Her eagerness to help him out with Sean, to pick up the groceries, to do the cleaning in here that he should have done himself, all said clearly she still had a crush on him.

He rubbed his hand over his eyes, blocking out the sight of her and hoping it would block out his thoughts. No such luck. When he lowered his hand and cleared his throat, she finally turned to face him again.

"I wasn't thinking," he said. Well, he was, but right then he definitely didn't have his focus on a topic he could share with her. He cleared his throat once more and started again. "It's Friday night."

For a moment, those dark eyes of hers lit up, confirming he'd been right about her feelings. Even as he congratulated himself for that, he cursed himself for not being more careful about what he'd said. She still had that schoolgirl crush, and those bright eyes gave her away. She thought he was about to ask her out.

He hated to dash her hopes. But it wasn't in her best interests—or his—for him to lead her on.

"It's still early yet," he said. "You should go. You probably have somewhere else you want to be tonight."

She shook her head. "Not really."

He crossed the room and plucked the dust cloth from her hand. "All right, then, you must have something else you want to do on a Friday night besides clean dusty shelves. Like hang out at the Bowl-a-Rama. Or go for a treat at the Big Dipper."

She gave him a slow smile that made him wish he'd stayed where he was. "I could go for something, but I sure don't need any ice cream to make my jeans even tighter."

Damn. He clutched the cloth, his fingers itching. And it had nothing to do with any dust allergy, that was for sure. He wanted to reach out and touch those curves he'd had the pleasure of seeing.

She couldn't have caught him watching her, could she? He glanced at the shelves. No mirrored surfaces, and even the rows of porcelain knickknacks, now freshly dusted, couldn't reflect an image from across the room.

No, Ally was just being Ally. A kid—now a woman— with a teasing sense of humor.

He had to believe that, because he refused to let himself think of her as anything more, as anything to him personally but an acquaintance. A babysitter. An employee.

He stepped back and cleared his throat again. *Get a grip.*

"Well," he said, "if you're not in the mood for an ice-cream treat, maybe you'd like a cold drink or two somewhere." He forced a laugh. "You already turned down the Bowl-a-Rama, and we know in Cowboy Creek on a Friday night, you don't get better than that or the Cantina. That might be an option. They still have the Friday dances there, don't they?"

He blocked out the vision of her dancing in front of the bookshelves.

Without a hint of a smile now, she nodded. "Yes, they do. And since you're in for the night, I guess I'll pack it in, too. I'll see you bright and early tomorrow."

"Bright and early?"

"It's Saturday, remember? Mrs. Browley mentioned the meeting, didn't she?"

He nodded. "Yeah. I forgot."

No, he'd been too distracted to think straight. And

he'd imagined this had been the longest week of his life. But it seemed it wasn't over yet.

Mrs. B *had* called last night to inform him of the spur-of-the-moment change in plans. She was taking Saturday off and wanted to let him know she had made arrangements with Ally to fill in for her.

Ally would be here at the ranch tomorrow.

With him and Sean.

All day long.

Chapter Five

From where he stood inside the barn, Reagan heard the hum of an approaching car's engine, followed by the slam of a door. Not Ally's. Her small car was neither that loud nor that solid.

He frowned. When had he taken note of the sound of her car?

"It looks like we've got company," he told Sean.

He crossed to the worktable in the corner, where he'd left the baby in his seat. It had been foolish, maybe, to come out here with Sean so soon after breakfast, but he had forgotten to clarify what Ally had meant by "bright and early." Sitting around the house waiting for her… waiting for *his son's babysitter* had made him antsy.

Not that he should have been sitting, with all he had to do inside. "Guess I need to stop avoiding the house," he said to Sean.

He hadn't been out here long enough to get his clothes dirty, but he scrubbed his dusty hands at the small sink. He tried not to think about dust…and last night…and, yet again, about Ally. Those images had led to new reasons he had been staying away from the house.

Jed Garland appeared in the barn doorway. "Morning." The older man looked around the interior of the barn and must have spotted the lumber Reagan had stacked near one wall. "Got enough there to build another barn, don't you? It's been a while since Cowboy Creek had a barn raising. Maybe we need to schedule one."

"Not for me. The new owner might be interested. Speaking of interest, how do you feel about a coffee?"

"I'm always ready for a cup."

Reagan picked up Sean in his carrier, and he and Jed left the barn.

"They say it's going to be a hot one today," Jed said. "You might want to take care about not overdoing the outside work. And not having the baby with you."

"Ally will be here soon to take care of him."

"Good thing. And how's that working out?"

"Fine." The effort to convince himself of that had him saying the word with more force than necessary. Judging by Jed's sudden smile, the man might have taken the emphasis as enthusiasm. Reagan tempered his response by adding, "I was lucky enough to be able to get Mrs. B to watch him, too."

"So Nan tells me."

"You've talked with Mrs. B?"

"Well, of course. I see her almost every time I run into town to Sugar's."

That made sense. SugarPie's bakery and sandwich shop was the hub of Cowboy Creek. "Mrs. B's with Sean for most of the time. Ally only sits with the baby for a while late in the day."

"That all did work out well, then, didn't it?"

Not very well. But he couldn't say that to Jed, who looked as pleased about the situation as if he'd had a hand in arranging it. For a moment, Reagan considered the idea Jed *had* gotten involved in his babysitting dilemma. But that was impossible, even for the man who knew everything in town.

As they neared the house, Jed said, "Before I forget, I'm here for more than a cup of coffee. Everybody out at the ranch wants the chance to catch up with you and to meet the baby. At breakfast, they all told me they'd have my hide if I didn't get you to come out tomorrow. The dining room is busy for brunch, but on Sundays we have an early dinner, and we'll have plenty of time then to sit and chat."

"That would be great. Sean and I will be there." Having something to do for part of the day would help distract him from…other things.

In the kitchen, he set the carrier on one side of the table and gestured the older man to a seat. "The coffeemaker's already primed." All he needed to do was hit the switch and grab a couple of mugs. "Milk? Sugar?" He had both, thanks to Ally volunteering to pick up groceries.

Jed waved a hand. "Black's fine by me."

"Talking about a new owner a few minutes ago reminded me, have you heard of anyone interested in this place yet?"

The sound of another car door slamming was quickly followed by footsteps on the wooden porch and then a knock on the kitchen door. He hurried across the room to swing the door open.

Ally stood on the porch. To his dismay, he suddenly realized how much he'd looked forward to seeing her again.

Today she wore a bright pink and red and orange

blouse along with her gold earrings and bracelets. And another well-fitting pair of jeans. Abruptly, he shifted his gaze to the sacks she held in one hand. "You stopped at SugarPie's," he said inanely.

"I did. And the L-G. And…uh…since I *am* bearing gifts—" she hefted the sacks and a plastic cooler "—mind if I come in?"

Dang. He stepped back a pace. As she passed him, he caught the scents of cinnamon and a light, spicy perfume. He went toward the counter, hoping that inhaling the scent of the brewing coffee would help him regain his focus.

"Hi, Jed," Ally said. "I saw your truck, so I knew you were here. Looks like I'm just in time for a midmorning snack." She went to the cupboard and took down another mug, a platter and several small plates. Reagan took her mug to fill it, too. "And you'll both be happy to know I've brought some of Sugar's sweet rolls."

"None for me," Jed said. "You won't have picked up enough for three."

"No worries. Sugar told me she put a few extra in the sack. It's almost like she knew you'd be here. After all, *everybody* knows her sweet rolls are your favorite."

Jed laughed. "That's Sugar for you—like Paz, always ready to feed a crowd." As Ally joined them at the table, he turned to Reagan. "You were wanting to know if I'd had anyone asking about the ranch yet. Not a word."

"You talked to the owners on either side of me?" He should have done that himself, but he'd felt oddly reluctant to discuss a sale with his parents' old friends.

"Yeah. No luck with them, either. But I'm sure someone will have an interest in the property. It's a nice spread, just the right size to be run by a couple of good men."

"My dad handled it on his own," he blurted, then wished he could take back the words. Jed hadn't meant anything by his statement. Ally's unblinking gaze didn't signify anything, either.

"Your daddy managed alone," Jed agreed, "but I think in the end it got to be too much for him. He wasn't the young man you are." Below his white eyebrows, his blue eyes stared steadily at Reagan.

Evidently, Jed *had* meant something by his previous statement.

"From what I hear at the store," Ally said, "property around Cowboy Creek hasn't moved too quickly lately. First of all, there hasn't been much activity. Most people who live here tend to stay here."

Was that another dig at him?

He gripped his mug and focused all his attention on swallowing his coffee without choking. Had Jed and Ally both decided to gang up on him, to get back at him for selling the place? For not supporting his parents like he should have? He didn't need anyone loading on the guilt about that. He had enough of his own.

"And then," Ally continued, "even if people are looking to buy, you might not get any takers."

She sounded hopeful that he wouldn't.

Of course. He should have remembered.

She, at least, wasn't coming up with reasons to make him feel bad about his actions. She wanted him to stay. Considering what he'd figured out last night about her crush on him, her hope that he might stick around wasn't surprising. But he couldn't let her believe he would satisfy that hope.

He set his mug firmly on the table. "If I can't find anybody local to take the place, I'll contact a few real estate agencies and put announcements in some of the bigger trade magazines. There's plenty of well-maintained equipment—large and small—out in the barn. I can either throw that in with the property to sweeten the deal, or reduce the asking price and sell the equipment off piecemeal to other ranchers in the area."

"Everybody around here is pretty well set," she said. "We sell heavy equipment through the store, too, and we don't get too many orders."

She had all the answers. Or thought she had.

He stared from her to Jed and back again. Whatever the reasons behind everything they had said, he couldn't let their opinions affect him. He shrugged. "If nothing else, I'll put the place up for auction. It'll go, sooner or later. And in any case, I'll already be gone."

ALLY PRESSED HER lips together, trying to keep from venting her frustration to the baby. Reagan couldn't have made his determination to leave Cowboy Creek any plainer if he'd written it in the dust on the windowsill in this living room.

Glaring, she swiped at the offending layer of grime.

If she planned to make any headway with him, she would have to move fast. Meanwhile, she needed something to keep her busy.

She looked at Sean, across the room in his baby carrier. She had begun to enjoy having the baby follow her with his eyes whenever she went near him. But she couldn't depend on Sean to occupy her completely. The child had to nap sometime. And considering Reagan was paying her to babysit, he would probably think providing entertainment was part of *her* job.

She certainly couldn't look for any assistance from him.

"Need some help?"

At the sound of his voice, she shrieked and grabbed at the canister of furniture polish her out-flung hand had just knocked off the chair beside her. She turned to face him. "Not again, Reagan." She rolled her eyes. "Does it give you a lot of pleasure to know you can scare the pants off me?"

Only after she blurted the question did she realize how it might come across if he took it literally—but of course, he wouldn't.

First of all, since his return, he had never even noticed she had grown up. His crack last night about the "ice-cream treat" proved it. Okay, she had always loved spending her entire weekly allowance at the Big Dipper in town. But did Reagan really think she seemed *that* young?

And another thing. Just like years ago, he barely seemed to notice when she was around. Even this morning, when she had arrived on his doorstep, his sweeping glance had gone right over her to the sack from SugarPie's.

If all that wasn't bad enough, she could wallow in embarrassment at having him catch her in here last night, dancing like a fool.

"I thought you planned to head out to the barn once Jed left," she said.

"I intended to. But he reminded me it's going to be hot out there today. I thought I'd stay in here for a change. You look like you could use some help with the higher shelves."

"Are you trying to point out the fact that I'm so much shorter than you?"

"Are you?" he asked blandly. "I hadn't noticed."

Had she called it, or what? As much as he cared, she could be invisible. That had to change.

"Your help would be much appreciated," she said as easily as she could manage with her jaw clamped tight.

As he approached, she swallowed hard. The closer he got, the more she wanted to reach out and touch. She wanted him near her, and yet she didn't. She wanted *him*…and yet she wasn't ready to make the first move.

Until she figured out her strategy, it would be best to keep her distance. Dust cloth in hand, she headed toward the wooden storage cupboards on the opposite side of the room.

"If we're going to do this right," he said, "we need to get together."

She froze, then turned to look at him. "What?"

"Give me a hand here." He gestured to the built-in bookcases she had only half finished cleaning when he'd interrupted her last night. "It'll go easier if I hand things down to you. You can dust 'em, and I'll take care of the shelves."

"Okay." Reluctantly, she went to stand beside him. He stood taller by more than a foot, and his reach made him seem even taller. "No wonder you were so good on the basketball team."

He looked at her, frowning. "Where did that come from?"

Her face heated, and she wished she hadn't tied her hair back with her bandanna again. She could have tilted her head and let her curls hide her flaming cheeks. "I only meant, you've got long arms. That's a good thing when you're trying to make dunk shots, right?"

"Yeah, it is." Smiling, he reached out to hand her a stack of books.

Again she froze, this time to stare at his face. Instantly, that smile had brought back the boy she had always loved.

"Whoa," he said sharply. The books she had forgotten about were slipping from her grasp. He grabbed them before they could hit the floor. "Having quick hands is a good thing, too, when you're trying not to fumble a football." He laughed. "Guess you're lucky your favorite sport is telephone tag."

"Very lucky," she agreed. At least he had remembered her telling him that. "Although I've been known to drop my cell phone once in a while."

"Maybe you need to practice holding on to things."

"Maybe I do," she said thoughtfully.

Turning back to the bookcases, they worked in near-silence for a while. Reagan wiped down and polished the wood until it gleamed. She dusted the books and more knickknacks, handing them to him—one at a time for safety's sake—to return to the shelves.

"These bookcases look handmade," she said.

"They are." He didn't elaborate.

"Did your father make them?"

He nodded.

Frowning, she lapsed back into silence. When they reached the last few knickknacks, she gave conversation another try. She eyed the display, mostly horses and dogs. "Your mama had about as many dust collectors as mine does."

"Yeah," he said shortly. "We're done with the shelves."

Again, she frowned. Today wasn't the first time he had changed the subject when she had mentioned either of his parents. As curious as she was to know all about Reagan, she hadn't asked specific questions or attempted to pry. But he had responded even to her most casual comment with simply a nod or a shrug or a new topic. The only history he had shared voluntarily was to acknowledge that the photo pinned to the bulletin board in his room was his mama's favorite picture, from his family's trip to California.

Maybe she needed to find more photos.

Meanwhile, swallowing a sigh, she handed the last knickknack to him.

As he set it on the top shelf, the dust cloth he had been using slipped from his hand. It tumbled down to land on her forearm.

"Who's the fumbler now?" she asked pertly.

"Very funny." He grabbed the cloth and brushed at her arm.

His fingertips stroked her skin, warming her at the same time it sent a shiver through her. Her bangle bracelets collided with a soft clang. Her heartbeat set off a pounding in her ears.

And when she looked up again and saw him staring at her, her indrawn breath made the loudest sound of all.

"Wh-what's next on the list?" she asked.

He hesitated. She gripped the cloth in her hand so tightly, she could feel her fingernails shredding the material.

"Let's have lunch," he said.

Touching her had not been part of the plan.

Reagan sat back in his chair at the kitchen table and

glanced at Ally, who was pushing most of her lunch around on her plate.

He hadn't known he'd had a plan, let alone that it didn't include touching her. He'd had to make it up as he'd gone along.

She had been right earlier. Once he had seen Jed off after their morning break, he had intended to go out to the barn. Instead, somehow his feet had gotten turned around and taken him in the opposite direction.

Sure, he had thought it was long past time he started on the house, and yeah, he had known she would be there. Once he'd walked into the living room, he had decided he would work at a distance from her, while having the pleasure of seeing her in the same room.

The pleasure he was taking now.

A man could look all he wanted. That didn't mean he could—or should—touch.

That danged dusting cloth. If not for accidentally dropping it on her arm, he wouldn't have felt the warmth of her against his palm. He wouldn't be thinking of that again now, when his focus should be on the next task at hand—and not on putting his hands on her.

"What do you want to do next?" she asked.

He started, hoping she hadn't read his mind. He scrubbed his hand over his eyes—as if that would erase the images all those thoughts had put in his head.

He knew what he wanted to do next, and it wasn't a good idea at all.

She looked across the kitchen at the playpen. "The baby's still asleep. I don't think he'll have much of an opinion."

"Probably not. He usually lets me have my own way, anyhow."

Her gaze flashed toward him, then down at her plate. He focused on his own plate, too.

When they had come in here for lunch, he fed Sean and put him into the playpen for a nap. Ally made sandwiches from a fresh supply of bread and meat she had picked up this morning at the L-G. She served them with a spicy peppered salad she had brought from home.

Maybe it was that salad that had gotten him so hot.

"It makes the most sense to hit the living room again once we're done with lunch," he said. "Might as well finish things off in there. But first I'd like to finish this off." He gestured at the salad.

"You like it?"

"Yeah, it's great. You made it?"

She shook her head. "No, my mama did. She's a wonderful cook. Not as good as Paz at the Hitching Post—*oops*. Forget what I just said."

"It's forgotten. But how about you? Don't you cook, too?"

"Some. But my mama tends to rule the kitchen."

Her laugh made her dark eyes sparkle. A man could get lost in those eyes. A man who was interested in a relationship, that is. Not him.

Fighting to keep his thoughts on track, he reached for the plastic container she had left on the table. "Did you want more of this?" he asked.

"No. All yours."

It was a great-tasting salad. It was also nothing like his own mom would have made, but salad or soup along with a sandwich brought back to him many Saturday lunchtimes spent at this table. Not that he wanted to sit here and reminisce about days he'd never see again.

That ranked about as high on his agenda as contemplating things he couldn't do with Ally.

As SOON AS they had cleared up after lunch, Reagan took the vacuum cleaner from the hall coat closet. After he finished cleaning the inside of each of the windows, Ally used the vacuum attachment for the drapes and window blinds. A temporary fix, as they both agreed.

"I'll tackle the outside of the windows sometime later this week."

"You'll still be here for a while, then." She sounded eager.

He shrugged. "With all the drawers and closets and boxes to empty upstairs, I can see this week here could need to roll into two."

Thanks to him and his reluctance to do what he had to inside the house.

At SugarPie's, Ally had asked him what had brought him here now. He'd given her the first response to come to mind—he hadn't had the chance, which was true enough.

The rest of the answer he hadn't given Ally was, it had taken him this long to find the willpower to get here. He had too much bad history behind him to want to resurrect any of it.

For Sean's sake, he wanted to look forward, not back. But like it or not, he had to pack up all the memories before he could sell this place. It would take longer than he'd thought. And for good or bad, the additional days would give him more chances to be with Ally.

How long would it take him to find the willpower to stay away from her?

"You'll be able to get another week off from work?" she asked.

"Shouldn't be a problem. I've still got time coming to me." He'd had no other reasons lately to use it. And if he needed a few extra days, he'd work out a deal with his boss. "I've used some vacation hours taking Sean for his newborn checkups, and that's about it."

"I'll bet he does well at his appointments. He's a happy baby, and he's so good about taking his bottle."

"His weigh-ins have sure been proving that." He realized he was grinning at her like a fool and stopped instantly. "We should keep moving."

"Now the windows are done, what about starting on the cupboards on the other side of the room?"

He looked across at the handcrafted cabinets his dad had installed and shook his head. "Not today. They're enclosed. We won't need to worry about them holding too much dust." They already held too many memories he didn't want to face.

He set to work shifting furniture to give Ally access to the floor. If his gaze strayed her way every time she leaned over to run the vacuum into a tight spot, who could blame him? And who knew watching a woman clean house could be so sexy?

After mentally shaking his head at himself, he turned to burning up his excess energy by following in her wake, putting the furniture back into place as she finished with each area. The work took them the rest of the afternoon, but their efforts were making the place livable.

Somehow, the thought bothered him. Maybe because he wouldn't be the one living here.

Ally put her hands on her hips and turned his way, looking up at him with a smile of satisfaction.

He stood close enough to notice the thickness of the black lashes outlining her gleaming eyes. Golden earrings flashed against her tanned skin and dark brown curls. Her cheeks were pink again from a little makeup and a lot of exertion. Add in her pink and red and orange blouse and her red bandanna, and the total package made her the most colorful woman he'd ever known.

"We're done for now, I think," she said.

He'd been *done for* a while ago.

This close, he could see a smudge on one of her full, curved cheeks. He reached up with his free hand and brushed the smudge away. Her skin felt smooth and delicate under his rough thumb. The gleam in her eyes turned liquid.

That reaction shouted a warning for him to get away. He'd ignored his instincts months earlier and had lived to regret it. He wanted to follow them now. He tried to follow them now. But again, his feet took control, bringing him where he'd wanted to be for days now.

Instead of backing off from Ally as he should have, he moved a step closer.

Chapter Six

The stroke of Reagan's work-roughened thumb against her cheek made Ally's heart rate speed up. As he stepped closer, her heart started to race. If it began to beat any faster, she would soon be vibrating from head to toe.

He dipped his head and brushed his mouth against hers. Just that light touch left her lips tingling. Without a second's pause, she reached up—way up—to rest her hands on his shoulders. She had to touch him, to hold him, to know he was real.

And he was.

This was Reagan Chase.

After all her years of longing for him, Reagan was finally within her reach. Even better, he was kissing her. That kiss gave her the one thing she had always lacked, the one thing she had always needed to spice up her life—the hot, peppery, flavorful taste of Reagan's mouth on hers.

He slipped one arm around her, holding her close, making her aware of every place their bodies touched. She was just as aware when he lifted his head and let go of her to step away.

She looked at him, not realizing she had forgotten

to breathe until she was forced to gulp a mouthful of air. His gaze dropped to her blouse for a moment before returning to her face.

His face looked shell-shocked.

As if already reading the first warnings, her heart dropped into a sad, thumping beat.

"I was out of line," he said. "That was uncalled for."

Her defenses rose into place. She was Ally Martinez. The Girl Most Likely… She tilted her head and batted her lashes at him. "Well, I'd have called for something like that a long time ago if I had known it was on offer."

"It wasn't. It shouldn't have been."

"Why not? What's wrong with it? We're both consenting adults."

He backed another step and shoved his hands into his back pockets. More than likely, he had no idea the move accentuated the hard curves and planes of his chest.

"Reagan," she said, fighting to keep her tone light, "it was only a kiss. I'll bet you give them out by the dozen and throw in a few extra, the way Sugar does with her sweet rolls." She wanted to step forward again, as if they were dancing a cha-cha and it was her turn to chase him.

She would follow him anywhere.

But his expression told her he would refuse to lead.

His next words proved it. "I should go check on Sean. The sound of the vacuum might have woken him up."

"You mean *I* should go check," she countered. "It's what you hired me for, after all." When she moved past him, she couldn't keep herself from brushing up against him, from allowing herself one more touch. Just in case it was the last she would ever have.

As she went down the hall to the kitchen, she could

hear Reagan's footsteps behind her. He was chasing her now.

She wished.

Before she could cross the room to go to the playpen, his voice stopped her. "That's all right," he said.

She turned back. He hadn't moved beyond the doorway.

"I can see him from here," he explained. "He's sleeping soundly."

She nodded. "All right. Then what should we do next?"

"You should go."

She frowned. "It's not even suppertime yet. I thought I was on duty until the end of the night."

"When I'm working outside, yeah. But I'm inside tonight. I won't be doing anything that requires an extra pair of hands. And I'll be able to keep an eye on Sean myself."

Her heart started that slow, heavy thump again. "All right. Then I'll pick him up from Mrs. Browley's tomorrow afternoon, as usual."

"I'm keeping him home. It's Sunday. Mrs. Browley's day of rest."

She blinked, fighting her surprise. And more. Was this it? Had she already lost her chance with him? "It's not a day off for you. At least, not while you're here at the ranch. You said there's so much to take care of. You said you're in a hurry to finish up."

"I've got other things to do tomorrow," he said vaguely.

Other things that didn't include her.

"That's fine," she said briskly. "It's a busy day for me, too. After church, my parents and I go to either the Hitching Post or SugarPie's for brunch, and then I usually meet up with a few of my friends." She forced a smile. "I'll just get all my stuff together." She gathered the plastic container she had rinsed and left on the counter, her water bottle from the refrigerator, her bag and sunglasses from beside the radio.

Trying to hide her dismay at the way this day was ending, and not sure she could hold back frustrated tears, she refused to look at Reagan. She knew he still stood in the doorway. She could sense rather than see that he still had his gaze on her.

She reached for the magazines she had brought from home this morning. Then she dropped her hand, leaving the pile untouched. The magazines would stay. She would be back on Monday.

She glanced at the baby, then, finally, at Reagan. "I doubt it will get chilly down here, but in case Sean needs his blanket, it's upstairs on the dresser."

"I'll see to whatever he needs." The side of his mouth quirked for a second, as if he'd fought a smile. As if he found it amusing she might think she knew better than he did what his own child would need.

And what do you *need?*

She wanted to ask but couldn't make that move. Yet.

She took a deep breath and let it out again. "All right, I guess I've got everything. I'll see you on Monday."

To her relief, he nodded, though he didn't quite meet her eyes.

And again, her heart got another workout, this time when it seemed to swell inside her. The poor man was beating himself up for something he felt he shouldn't have done. Something she had wanted more than anything in the world.

Telling him that right now might only scare him away permanently.

He thought she still was nothing more than the

schoolgirl he'd paid no attention to years ago. She would have to prove to him how much she had grown up.

AT THE HITCHING POST, Reagan parked his truck beneath a tree near the corral. The shade would help keep the vehicle cooler.

Yesterday hadn't been as hot as Jed had heard in the weather reports. But now it was early in the afternoon, and in summertime in New Mexico, the heat was highest later in the day.

Across the yard, he could see Jed over near the barn.

After giving the man a wave, he leaned back inside the truck to transfer his son into the baby carrier. "Looks like we've got part of the reception committee waiting for us," he told Sean.

He had been grateful to wake up this morning and recall Jed's invitation to Sunday dinner at the hotel—especially after what had happened last night.

Giving in and kissing Ally had been a big mistake. The truth of that had become all too obvious the second he had wrapped his arm around her. Immediately following his body's uncontrollable response, his brain reacted, blasting out another warning.

Fortunately, that time, it acted like a slap of cold water to his senses.

After his relationship with Elaine, it would be a while—a good long while—before he'd hook up with another woman.

He needed to focus on the reason he'd come back to Cowboy Creek.

Again, Ally had been the levelheaded one in their conversation, reminding him he wanted to get the property ready for sale and be gone.

To do that, he would need to cut down on the time they spent together. She was too much fun to listen to, too much of a distraction. And while she might have been hell on some of his body parts, she was way too easy on his eyes and mouth.

Last night, after he had told her she could leave early, he had been surprised but relieved when she hadn't put up much argument.

He lifted the carrier out of the truck and grabbed the bag he used for Sean's baby stuff.

Funny, just two days ago, he'd broken into a sweat at the idea of having Ally with him at the house all day long. Now, he couldn't handle being there without her...

He swallowed a groan. He had spent a good part of last night wondering what might have happened if he hadn't backed away from her. Somehow, he had to stay away from those kinds of thoughts. Instead of wanting to hold her, he should be making sure he stayed well out of arm's reach.

"We'll be gone from Cowboy Creek again soon, Sean," he promised the baby.

As they crossed the yard and approached the ranch owner, Reagan looked around him and gave an approving nod. "It's been a while since I've been here, Jed, but except for the new signpost, the place seems to look just the way it always did."

One boot propped up on the corral fence rail, the older man chuckled and shook his head. "You'll be changing your tune once you get the grand tour. Did you hear we're back in the wedding business?"

"I saw Layne at Sugar's earlier this week. She mentioned Tina and your other granddaughters had all gotten married. I can see where three weddings in the family might have kept you busy. But I wouldn't call that a business."

"No, I meant more than that. We started off with my three girls getting hitched, but now we're catering outside weddings and receptions here again, too, just like we did years ago."

Reagan nodded. "I imagine your family is happy about that."

"They are, for sure." Jed glanced at Reagan's bare hands. "I take it you're not married."

He laughed shortly. "I already told Ally I'm not. And I'm sure she told Tina and that info worked its way back to you."

"It did," Jed said with a grin. "As it should have. I like to know what's going on in this town." He nodded toward Sean. "So what are your plans for this little one?"

"Plans? You mean after he grows up?"

"I mean when he starts looking for his mama."

"I'll take care of him."

I'll see to whatever he needs.

He had said that to Ally last night, after she had told him about leaving Sean's blanket upstairs. She wanted him to know where to find it in case Sean got cold.

Crazy, but that statement of hers had gotten to him. In that one sentence, she had thought more about the baby, had shown more concern for Sean than his own mother ever had.

But he still wasn't hooking up with another woman, even one who'd had a fleeting, concerned thought about his son.

"Sean won't need a mother," he said flatly to Jed. "He's got me."

The older man shrugged. "Son, a boy always needs his mama, for as long a time as he's lucky to have her."

A beat of silence went by. He thought of good memories overshadowed by bad ones.

"A few brothers and sisters would be a nice idea, too," Jed said.

Reagan didn't at all like where this conversation was headed. It sounded like Jed was fitting him for a family.

Ally would handle this with a laugh and a light reply. He tried to do the same. "You don't think I'm here to sign up for your wedding services, do you? If so, I hate to disappoint you, but I'm a confirmed bachelor."

Jed laughed, too. "If you think that, I've got a handful of grandsons-in-law you can talk to."

"No, thanks."

"Well, suit yourself." Jed consulted a silver pocket watch. "It's about time we head in for dinner. We'll have quite a few friends at the family table this afternoon. There's you and Sean, of course. And then Wes Daniels. You remember him, don't you?"

"Sure. He sat behind me alphabetically in grade school and always complained I was too tall for him to see the front of the classroom. But he caught up to me in high school. We were on the basketball and baseball teams together."

Jed nodded. "He's a widower now. Just lost his wife a year or so ago."

"I'm sorry to hear that."

"Yeah. It was rough on him and his kids, of course, and a big shock to us all. I've got his brother working for me now, and even Garrett has a hard time getting Wes to go anywhere much. It's all I can do to get him and the kids out here to the ranch for Sunday dinner once in a while. With the two of you being both friends and single dads, you should have a lot in common." They had reached the rear entrance of the hotel. "And then there's Ally."

"Ally?" He almost missed a step on his way up to the porch.

"Yeah. She's here for dinner, too. Tina invited her," Jed finished in a rush.

Reagan frowned. Maybe the man thought he'd accuse him of trying to bring him and Ally together. Then again, maybe he already *was* in there swinging.

Jed held the back door wide for him to carry Sean into the hotel. Remembering the layout of the place from previous visits here, he could have found the dining room on his own, blindfolded. Even if he hadn't known the way, the smell of Paz's good cooking would have directed him down this hall to the kitchen.

He thought of Ally comparing her mom's cooking to Paz's.

He thought of Ally way too often.

Jed closed the door behind them and began walking down the hall.

Reagan stayed in the entryway. He had looked forward to today's visit as a way to distract him from thoughts of Ally, a way to keep her face and body and voice from his mind. So much for that idea. And there was no way he could get out of this. Accepting the invitation to dinner here had committed him to spending the afternoon in her company.

A few feet down the hall, Jed stopped and turned back.

"It's all right, son," he called with a laugh, "you can come along. I'm not so old that you need to give me a head start."

A FEW MINUTES before dinnertime, Ally glanced around the Hitching Post's large dining room.

She had always loved the Old West decor of the hotel, the dark wooden tables and chairs, the wood and metal light fixtures above the tables, the Southwestern Native American and Mexican pottery sitting in niches or hanging from the walls. And after having eaten so many meals at the hotel, either here or in the big kitchen, she knew the routines.

The Garlands and their friends occupied the long table in the center of the dining room. Hotel guests took seats at the tables of various shapes and sizes scattered around the family table.

And before Sunday dinners, there was always some mingling, like a predinner cocktail party minus the cocktails.

During her mingling moments now, she laughed and smiled and, she was sure, acted perfectly normal—which for her meant making everyone believe she never had a care in the world. Behind the mask, her thoughts were quite a few miles away. With Reagan.

Since their kiss, he was almost all she could think about. She wondered how things would be between them when she went out to the ranch again tomorrow.

On the other side of the room Tina was chatting with a group of the hotel's guests. Ally saw her best friend glance in her direction, her expression puzzled.

The man standing beside Ally shifted his feet. Realizing she had let her mind wander for too long, she turned to Wes Daniels.

Wes had been a couple of years ahead of her in school, in Reagan's class. "How are the kids? You didn't bring them with you today?"

"They're doing fine. And I did bring them along. My kids and all of Jed's great-grandkids, except for Tina and Cole's new baby, are over at Pete and Jane's." Pete was Jed's ranch manager, and his wife, Jane, was Jed's oldest granddaughter. They lived in the manager's house on the property.

"I should have realized," she said. "It's so quiet in here—besides the adults talking, I mean."

He smiled briefly. She realized how infrequently he had smiled lately. And how infrequently anyone had seen him at all since his wife had died.

"Kids do make a lot of noise, don't they?" he asked.

Sean doesn't. Granted, other than when she visited the ranch, her time around children was limited to next to nothing. And Sean was just an infant. Still, he was the quietest baby she had ever seen.

Maybe that meant he didn't like her.

She couldn't let her mind go off in that direction. She had enough to worry about with his daddy, whose kiss certainly seemed to prove *he* liked her. A lot. Too bad that kiss told her one thing, but his actions said just the opposite.

A second glance from Tina told her she needed to get her thoughts back to where she was and the person she was with. "I've seen Garrett at the Cantina quite a bit lately." Wes's older brother was frequently one of her dance partners. "I don't see you in town very often, though." She rested her hand on Wes's arm. "How are you doing?" she asked quietly.

"Fine," he said. Short and simple and without any hint of emotion in his voice.

The way Reagan had sounded yesterday afternoon.

She tried her best but couldn't keep from replaying his words in her mind.

You should go.

She heard his voice again—only this time, it was here and now. She snapped her gaze to the doorway of the dining room.

Reagan stared back at her.

Her hand tightened reflexively on Wes's arm. To cover the reaction, she smiled at him and said brightly, "I think an old friend of yours just walked in. Have you seen Reagan Chase since he's been home?"

"No, I haven't. Didn't know he was back."

"Well, he is. And now's your opportunity." Her mask firmly in place, she turned to wave Reagan toward them.

Judging by his expression, he wasn't overjoyed to see her. She felt the same about seeing him.

Tomorrow afternoon would come soon enough, and she still hadn't had time to figure out what to do. At least here, surrounded by her friends, she wouldn't have to face him on her own.

Chapter Seven

"What do you think of my scheme now, girl?" Jed asked.

After their meal, folks had begun making their way to the sitting room just off the Hitching Post's lobby. Seeing Tina was going to be the last to leave the dining room, he had hung back, too.

They walked slowly down the hall together.

"Giving Ally lessons in taking care of a baby is one thing," she said in a low voice. "Helping you match her up with someone is another story. But I still don't have a problem with your plan—as long as she doesn't figure out I'm part of the planning committee."

He laughed.

They halted at the T where the hallway met the stairs and the lobby. Tina looked across the lobby toward the sitting room doorway. The sound of voices, Ally's among them, came from the room. But he knew his youngest granddaughter well, and he could see she continued to feel some concern. "What's got you troubled?"

"I don't know… I guess it's just, Ally doesn't seem like herself."

"She had a fine time at dinner, same as she always does, making us all laugh at almost everything she said. I'm glad to say she even got a few smiles out of Wes."

She nodded. "I saw, and I'm glad, too. But her own smile doesn't look right to me."

"Well, you know her best. We'll keep an eye on her. Let's get in there and see what's up."

"You go, *Abuelo*. I'll be there in a few minutes. I want to check on the baby."

"Sounds good."

He ambled toward the sitting room.

Inside the wide doorway, a glance and a quick listen informed him the hotel guests gathered in one corner were discussing tomorrow morning's trail ride. In a short while, he would move over there to take up his hosting duties, a task always more of a pleasure to him than a chore.

Meanwhile, he had some matchmaking to do. And that always pleased him equally well.

The family guests—Ally, Reagan and Wes—had taken over another corner of the room. Ever since Tina and Ally had become friends, Ally had spent almost as much time here in the hotel as she did at her own home. He took a fast but close look at her. Maybe Tina had been right about the girl not behaving like herself.

The trio in the corner sat on a couple of the comfortable couches grouped in that area, but Ally's stiff posture didn't make her seem the least bit at ease.

Reagan's expression had him coming in a close second.

Only Wes, who had taken one couch by himself, and Reagan's baby, in his seat between Ally and Reagan, looked completely relaxed.

Jed fought to hide a smile.

When two young folks looked that uncomfortable in a crowd, their chance of loosening up with each other often improved once they were alone. Nothing he could do about that now, short of clearing out the entire hotel. But he had other means of helping the situation.

He crossed the room. After nodding at the trio in greeting, he clapped Wes on the shoulder. "Young man, I've been looking for a chance to talk with you. Can you spare me a few minutes of your time?"

"Sure."

As Wes rose, Jed smiled a farewell to Ally and Reagan.

REAGAN FELT SOME envy as he watched the two men walk out of the sitting room.

Why couldn't he have been the one Jed had wanted to talk to?

Then again, maybe that wouldn't have been the best thing, if his conversation with the older man only continued to run along the lines it had before dinner. Weddings and marriages... Babies and their moms...

Not one of them a topic he wanted to discuss.

Still, considering the way his willpower had deserted him yesterday, it definitely wasn't a good thing to be left sitting here on this couch with Ally.

"Dinner was great, wasn't it?" she asked. It was the first thing she had said to him directly since he had arrived.

"Yeah," he answered.

That he could agree with. But all through the meal, he had the sensation of a boulder dropping into the pit of his stomach, a reminder of the way he'd felt when he had walked into the dining room and spotted Ally with her hand on another man's arm. When she had then turned deliberately and smiled at that other man.

The trouble was, he had no cause to have that feeling. As Ally herself had said last night, their kiss was just a kiss. He had no claims on her, and she had none on him. And that was exactly how things needed to stay.

"Cat got your tongue?" she asked teasingly.

She had left her hair loose today. No bandanna holding back her tumbling curls. She swept a fall of those curls over her shoulder, and another boulder hit the pit of his stomach.

During dinner, he had listened to her talk and laugh. Once, he had seen her tug at her hair, probably without realizing it. He had watched her brush her napkin with her palms to smooth it across her lap. Every sound and every movement had driven him a little more crazy.

Thinking about her that way was completely insane.

She raised her eyebrows and stared at him.

"What?" he blurted, hoping she hadn't read his thoughts.

"I asked if the cat had your tongue." She smiled. "It's an expression we use around here. It means—"

"Very funny. You know we both know what it means."

"Well, maybe so. But I thought all your years in the big city might have made you forget."

"No, it didn't. And you didn't give me much chance. You were doing enough talking and laughing for both of us. *And* Wes."

Abruptly, her smile disappeared. "Wes doesn't have a lot to laugh about lately. Neither do his kids." She ran her hand along the edge of Sean's carrier and sat silently.

Finally, she said in a low voice, "Wes's kids don't have a mama, either."

She hadn't come right out and asked about Sean's mother—about his ex—but he could hear the hint of a question in her statement.

He was struggling not to think about this woman sitting beside him. He couldn't tell her the woman he'd thought he'd loved had dropped him without a second's hesitation.

Instead, he kept the conversation on Wes Daniels. "Jed told me he had lost his wife not long ago."

She nodded. "Yes. From cancer. She was gone almost as soon as they found out. It happens that way with so many people."

"Like my mom." The words were out before he could stop them.

"I know," she said sympathetically.

She would know. Everyone in town did. If there was one thing Cowboy Creek could be depended upon, it was sharing news—bad or good—and pulling together to support one of their own.

Sean stirred in his sleep and gave a little startled cry.

He reached for his son at the same time Ally did, and their hands brushed in the air over the baby. She pulled her hand back and rested it in her lap.

Sean began to wail.

"He's overtired, a couple of naps behind where he should be for the day." He took his son from the carrier and settled him against his shoulder, patting the baby's back with his free hand.

He thought again of Ally saying she had left his son's blanket upstairs.

More things he didn't want to acknowledge nudged at him.

He needed to get out of here.

Sean let out one of his more strident cries.

Good baby, always willing to help Daddy.

He rose from the couch and grabbed the infant seat.

"I should go," he told Ally. He didn't miss the irony. She probably hadn't, either.

Those were nearly the same words he had said to her yesterday.

WHEN ALLY PARKED outside the ranch house with Sean on Monday afternoon, she took him with her directly to the barn. Somehow, she knew that was where she would find Reagan.

They had made good progress in the living room on Saturday. Together. But after the way he had dismissed her that afternoon…and then considering how he had run off from the Hitching Post at the first opportunity yesterday…

Well, she knew better than to expect he would be ready and willing to play house with her again.

And she was right.

As she reached the barn, she heard the screech of metal scraping metal. She came to a stop in the doorway and surveyed the area in amazement. Reagan had more parts and equipment spread out over every horizontal surface than the hardware store had in stock.

"What happened?" she asked. "It looks like a wrecking crew went to work in here."

He wouldn't meet her eyes. "I'm getting some of the equipment ready to sell."

Her heart jumped to her throat. She tightened her grip on the baby carrier. "You have a buyer for the property?"

"No. But in case it takes a while to find someone who's interested, I may go ahead and put some of this up for sale separately."

"Oh. Well, if you need anything, Sean and I will be in the house."

"Yeah. I'll be out here for a couple of hours, at least."

"I can see that." She had *hoped* for that. She needed time to put her plan into action.

She went back to her car and retrieved the sacks and the cooler she had left tucked on the floor behind the driver's seat. "Your daddy can hide out in the barn for as long he likes," she told the baby. "But whatever time he decides to come in for the night, he's going to get a *big* surprise."

Inside the house, she set his carrier on the table while she stored the contents of the cooler in the refrigerator.

Then she settled Sean in his playpen, where he lay looking up, his blue eyes fixed on her. Going to her knees in front of the playpen, she crossed her arms on the padded rail and rested her chin on her arms.

"Okay," she began, "this is the deal. I'm going to be just a *teeny* bit deceitful with your daddy. But don't you worry. Everything will work out all right. You'll see. He and I get along well, Sean. I mean, *really* well."

Her face heated, partly from the memory of what had happened between her and Reagan in this house, partly from the knowledge that she planned to share the details with his one-month-old son. "The other night, you weren't in the living room with us, but your daddy kissed me." She nodded emphatically. "Yes, he did. And, oh, my, *what* a kiss—"

She snapped her mouth closed and cleared her throat. "I'll stop with that. There's such a thing as too much information."

And there were some things she couldn't put into words. No matter what Reagan had said about being out of line with her and his action being uncalled for, the truth was, it had happened. He had kissed her. And she couldn't miss the way his body responded. She couldn't misunderstand what the reaction meant. He had enjoyed that kiss as much as she had. No matter how much he protested or pretended to believe she was still too young for him, he was interested.

"So that's what happened," she said to Sean. "Never mind the play-by-play—and that's a sports term your daddy will explain to you someday—but for now, just trust me. That kiss proved what I'm telling you. He and I get along."

She smiled. "And tonight, we're going to get along a lot better."

A COUPLE OF hours later, Ally attempted to light a tall white candle with a match that bobbed and shook and went out in her hand.

She struck another match and tried again. She had to get these candles lit.

"When you're planning a seduction," she told Sean, "you need to set the right mood." She shot a look across the room at him in his infant seat. "But don't go getting any ideas, you hear me? You're way too young to think about seducing a girl."

Finished with the lighting ceremony, she waved her hand, gesturing at the candles and pewter holder she had brought from home, the china and glasses and silverware she had found in the dining room hutch here and had washed in the kitchen sink, and the vase of hot-pink and flaming-red tulips she had picked up at the L-G Store.

"What do you think, baby? Is it all a go?"

She walked over to stand beside him. To be safe, she had placed his seat on one of the sturdy pine captain's chairs from the kitchen set, which she had moved far away from the candles on the table.

As she looked down, Sean shifted his arm.

"Oh, you think it deserves a fist bump, huh?" She reached over to touch her knuckles to his tiny hand. "Thanks for the vote of confidence."

For a moment, her own confidence began to flicker like the flames on the candles. Then she lifted her chin and stiffened her spine. With her arms held straight out at her sides, she twirled once slowly in front of Sean. "And what do you think of this?"

When she looked down at him again, his eyes had closed. He had drifted off to sleep.

"Great," she whispered. "I hope that's not your way of telling me what to expect with your daddy."

She walked over to the kitchen sink. It was just dark enough outside for the east-facing window above it to provide a reflection against the glass. She looked at the slightly hazy outline of herself and nodded in satisfaction. "Not too bad."

The reflection showed her from the waist up. She couldn't see her shoes but knew the heels gave her a couple of extra inches of height. She couldn't see the lower half of her knit dress but could feel the hem of it snuggling against her, a few inches above her knees.

She *could* see the top of the dress, with its wild bright pattern, gauzy short sleeves and deep V of a neckline. In the light from the kitchen the silver chain she wore sparkled, and the little silver tassel hanging from the chain dangled just above the V.

V for victory… She smiled.

Through the window, she saw Reagan exit the barn. Tall and broad-shouldered, he walked in that loose-limbed, easy way he always had. Whether he was running down a court or field or just walking across the school cafeteria, he always seemed comfortable and in control.

Her reminiscing had left her standing still by the sink. Reagan had almost reached the house. She stumbled back a step, catching one heel on the floor mat and almost tripping over her own feet.

"Settle down, girl," she said, sounding like a cowhand from Garland Ranch trying to calm one of Jed's mares. The thought made her break into a nerve-induced giggle.

Then the kitchen door opened and the giggle died.

Reagan stepped into the room. He took one look at her and froze.

With her hands as shaky as when she'd tried to light the candles, she ran her palms down her hips, pretending to smooth her dress, attempting to flirt with him without saying a word.

His gaze followed, running down her body.

She swallowed a satisfied smile. "I hope you're hungry."

His gaze shot to hers again. He sat heavily on the bench by the door.

Oh, yeah, that's interest. Just don't scare him away.

"Hungry for supper, I mean," she said lightly. "I made lasagna. Mexican lasagna. Nice and spicy." Truthfully, she'd more or less watched Mama make it. But a woman couldn't spill all her secrets. And, of course, she would have mastered the recipe by the *next* time she served the dish to Reagan.

"I ate a late lunch," he said, his tone flat.

She froze. *Maybe there won't even be a* this *time.*

And that was the worst excuse to miss a meal she had ever heard.

The double *thunk* as his boots landed on the floor might have been the sound of her heart, broken in two and dropping inside her chest.

Almost, she wanted to roll her eyes at her own dramatic thought. Only almost, because she wasn't quite sure it was all drama.

How hard would it have been for him to say yes? To make an attempt? To offer the slightest bit of encouragement? To give her a chance?

Those questions threatened to burst from her, but somehow she managed to hold them back.

Just as she had earlier when her confidence had threatened to desert her, she lifted her chin and stiffened her spine. She might not have Reagan, but she had pride… even if it *had* taken a beating. "No problem. Supper will be all mine…and I'm a *big* fan of nice and spicy."

That snapped his gaze to hers again. Then he looked down—but not away. He started at her shoes, moved up her legs to her dress, lingered on that victorious V and the tassled necklace, rose to her face. Every inch his gaze traveled felt as warm and intimate as a physical caress.

He looked at the table she had set with the candles, the china and glassware, the flowers.

Then he looked back at her and shrugged. "Seems like you went to a lot of effort." He cleared his throat. "I need a good shower. By the time I'm done, I could probably go for a bite."

Chapter Eight

Forget the bite. He wanted the full meal.

Reagan gripped his fork and attempted to focus on his plate. He'd needed a good shower, all right. And he had taken one. A good, long, cold shower—and it still wasn't enough to cool him down.

The "nice and spicy" lasagna wasn't helping, either.

Neither was Ally in that outfit she'd worn. That first sight of her when he'd walked into the kitchen had floored him, and while he would never admit his legs had given out, he'd been thankful for the bench near the door.

Every move she made pulled the stretchy fabric of her dress tight in one place or another. A couple of her go-rounds with the pepper shaker over her plate had left him breaking out in a sweat.

"Don't you like the lasagna?" she asked. "You haven't eaten much of it."

"I'm savoring," he said truthfully. But as good as the dish tasted, that wasn't what he'd referred to.

He had to fight to tear his gaze from her and transfer it to his plate. And as good as she looked, that wasn't what had hit him hardest of all.

What had done him in was the sight of her with her

shoulders squared and her chin tilted up. A defensive stance.

Against him.

She had come on to him and he'd tried his best not to acknowledge the fact—in his conversation with her, anyhow. His body had already made its own response clear.

She had gone to a lot of trouble to make dinner something special, and he'd turned down her invitation. The least he could have done was take her up on the meal.

So he'd changed his mind, then gone upstairs to shower and change his clothes. And now look where it had gotten him. Sitting across the candlelit table from Ally. Those candles made her eyes sparkle. Made her hair shine. Made that little silver tassel dangling just above the V of her dress shimmer every time she so much as took a breath.

He struggled to take a gulp of air.

"Had enough?" she asked.

"Not nearly enough." His voice sounded strangled. He forked up another piece of the lasagna. "I mean, this is good stuff. I could eat the entire tray of it myself." Even in the candlelight, he could see her cheeks flush at the compliment. "Maybe you should go into business making and selling it."

"Maybe not." But she laughed.

That silver tassel danced. It reminded him of the afternoon he'd found her dancing in the living room. He inhaled heavily again and focused on his meal. Along with the lasagna, she had made a green salad and dinner rolls. Everything tasted great, and luckily, the fork and the rolls kept his hands occupied. If only he could say the same about his mind.

He needed a diversion. Conversation would have to do.

"If you're not going into the food industry," he said, "do you plan to stay in hardware and feed?"

"I might. The job has a lot of perks. It's close to home, fairly easy work and I meet a lot of nice people. I sometimes complain about the pay, but let's face it, there aren't a lot of places to spend money in Cowboy Creek, anyway. Unless you hit the Bowl-a-Rama."

"Or the Big Dipper."

For some reason, that made her roll her big brown eyes. "Or there."

"Not much of an internet shopper?" His ex was. They had shared a credit card account, and long story short, that was one thing he didn't miss.

"Oh, no. Not me. You can't make sure you'll get the right size if you order something from a website. When I go shopping, I want to try everything on. Like this dress." She raised both hands held wide, palms up, and the stretchy material stretched. The tassel shivered.

So did he. He tore his gaze away and went back to his meal.

"Um…I think the flowers are part of the pattern," she said, indicating his empty plate. "Want seconds?"

He shook his head.

"Then if you're done, I'll take that."

And he'd get to sit back and watch her walk to the sink. He'd never survive the pleasure. He shot to his feet and grabbed the plate and the empty basket from the rolls. "I'll help clear. It's the least I can do, considering you made such a nice meal."

"I'm glad you enjoyed it."

They set the plates in the sink, and she turned to rest

one hip against the edge of the counter. "I hope you saved room for something sweet."

Dang. He would never survive standing this close to her, either.

He was having a heckuva time trying to keep his gaze and his hands to himself. And that was her intention. He might have screwed up reading the signs in his previous relationship, but he wasn't a complete idiot. Ally was leading him on.

It was why she'd cooked dinner for him tonight. Why she'd made her hair even curlier, worn the spicy perfume and heels and short stretchy dress and, he'd be willing to bet, even why she'd picked that particular necklace with the shimmying tassel.

Her plan was to get him to want her.

She'd succeeded.

He reached up to run his finger down one long curl that dangled almost to her waist.

"Ally…"

He'd tried to resist. He'd definitely tried. More than once. Claiming he didn't have an appetite. Telling the truth about needing that shower. One more strike, and he'd be out of this game. But she was serving him a meal in his own candlelit kitchen, and she was dressed to thrill and obviously ready to start something and…

And his willpower couldn't hold out.

He touched her cheek. She turned to him, settling her hands on his shoulders and her body against his. Her willing response confirmed it—he'd been right about everything he'd said to himself about her intentions.

What he'd forgotten was to remind himself this was all wrong.

"Ally." He took her hands from his shoulders and

held her fingers lightly. She looked up at him, starry-eyed in the candlelight, and he almost lost his nerve. "I think we'd better have some dessert."

She gave him a throaty laugh. "This *is* dessert."

Whoa.

"You've planned everything, haven't you?" He shook his head. "I'm sorry, but I'll need to skip this course. For sure, you're as sweet as any dessert could be. And in that dress you are one hell of a temptation. But this wouldn't work out, for either of us. As much as I don't like saying it, you're a temptation I'll have to fight to resist."

He hated seeing the sparkle leave her eyes and seeing that she, the girl who always had a good comeback, now had nothing to say.

But if he took the dessert she offered, he'd hate himself even more.

Worse, tomorrow, so would she.

ALMOST TWENTY-FOUR hours later, Ally still couldn't believe she had so completely messed up. Reagan had turned down...everything she had offered. And she had made a fool of herself.

She was lucky to have gotten herself home from the ranch in one piece last night.

She wasn't so lucky to be sitting here this afternoon, in the waiting room of Cowboy Creek's only women's health practice. But in a call to Tina that morning, she had learned her best friend had a follow-up visit with the baby's doctor. And Ally had a need to talk to her best friend.

Or maybe a need to delay her trip out to the ranch after work.

On her way to meet Tina, she had picked up Sean at Mrs. Browley's house, and there her luck had changed. Sort of. Mrs. Browley informed her Reagan had left a message for her. He would be working out on the ranch all day and would be late getting in at the house.

He could have called her cell phone. That first day when they'd met at SugarPie's, she had given him her number in case he needed to reach her. But obviously, after last night, he expected to feel as much awkwardness as she did when they spoke again.

"I was sorry we didn't have a chance to talk on Sunday," Tina said, "or to catch up until now."

In the waiting room, they had taken seats in chairs placed between an oversize potted plant and the door to the examining rooms in the rear of the office. Both of these separated them from the rest of the patients in the room, which helped give the illusion of privacy. But it was only an illusion.

Ally kept her voice low. "I was sorry, too."

"What's going on? I could tell at dinner something was bothering you. Then you left so soon after Reagan took Sean home, I didn't even know you were gone until *Abuela* mentioned you had said goodbye."

Across the room, a child Ally guessed to be about two, and who looked almost as frustrated as she felt, was having a tantrum.

Tina gave her a small smile. "And I'm sorry about having to meet here."

"Don't worry. After the day I had yesterday, what's a little more torture?"

Tina stared at her. "What happened?"

"Nothing happened. Nothing *is* happening. That's the point. I wanted to try to get Reagan to…to loosen up with me a little more, so I made him a nice supper last night."

"You cooked for him?" Even her best friend couldn't hide her surprise.

"If you're worried I've killed him off, don't be. No, I did not cook for him. He thought I did…but I brought over one of Mama's lasagnas."

"Oh." Tina smiled. "Well, you *could* have made that yourself, if you'd wanted to. *Abuela* taught Jane, and even she said it's a piece of cake."

"The food was only step one," she blurted. "I *dressed up* for Reagan to make sure he'd want to *get up* to something after dinner, and he…" She darted a glance around the room, then looked back at Tina and forced a laugh. "Well," she murmured, "let's just say, at this rate, I'll never have to worry about needing a pediatrician."

"Oh, Ally," Tina said, not even attempting to hide her sympathy.

"It doesn't matter. You already know how babies feel about me. And how I feel about them." She adjusted the edge of Sean's sleeve. When his eyes blinked open, she smiled down at him and stroked his cheek.

"Ally," Tina said, "you remember when you were always telling me I needed to lighten up and brighten up—"

"Of course I remember." She smiled at the memory, too. "I was trying to be helpful, *chica*. Color's a beautiful thing."

"I know you were. And you even managed to change my mind about it." Tina nudged her with her elbow. "See? I'm wearing a pink shirt."

Ally rolled her eyes. Granted, she was the one who loved bright, bold clothes and jewelry and everything else, but Tina had always worn some colors…along with her boring beiges and tans. "You're just showing me that shirt to try to make me feel better."

"Why wouldn't I? You lighten up and brighten up everyone's lives."

"Obviously not Reagan's. *But…?* Come on, I can hear it in your voice."

"But…well, maybe light and bright isn't what he needs."

"Why? You suspect the man's color-blind?"

"Be serious for once," Tina said softly. "I'm just saying, neither of us knows what's happened in Reagan's life since he left Cowboy Creek." Automatically, they both looked down at Sean. "We don't know anything about the mother of his baby, or where she is, or why she's not with them."

"They're not together. I know that, at least. You remember, I told you he said he's not married. Besides, he ki—" She snapped her mouth shut. He might have turned her down last night, but the other day, he *had* kissed her. And liked it.

Tina eyed her.

She sighed. "You're not going to let that almost-slip slide, are you? Fine. The truth is, a couple of days ago, he kissed me. A kiss says he's interested. Right?"

Tina looked troubled. "It might. But most guys are interested in making out, given half the chance."

A few feet away, a baby let out an impatient cry, instantly setting off a chain reaction. Ally felt tempted to join in. With all the noise, who would notice?

"That's the thing," she said, almost whispering now despite the chaos surrounding them. "I *did* give him a chance to make out with me. And to do a lot more.

And he didn't go for it." She forced a laugh. "Unbelievable, huh?"

"It's his loss." Tina lowered her voice even more. "You're my BFF, Ally. I know you better than anyone. And I know, back when we were in junior high, you only turned yourself into a flirt in the first place because you wanted Reagan Chase to notice you."

"Well, I fizzled out then," she said. "But I sure failed spectacularly last night."

"And that's my point. If he doesn't like you the way you are, then he doesn't deserve you."

"That's the problem, Tina. He does like me. He said so. But for some reason—probably connected to whatever happened to him while he was gone—he's fighting it."

"Well, then...your advice to me basically boiled down to trying something else. Maybe that would be worth a shot."

Ally thought for a few moments, then shrugged. "It couldn't hurt, could it?"

This time, they both laughed.

ALLY SPENT A long afternoon and evening alone with Sean.

By the time she had gone upstairs to change the baby and put him into his pajamas, there was still no sign of Reagan. She had begun to worry something might have happened to him out on the ranch. Whether or not the man wanted her didn't matter. She would still be concerned for his safety.

She couldn't say any of that aloud. Sean was very easy to talk to, but she had to be careful what she said to him. She didn't want him to hear anything negative from her about Reagan.

"Maybe I should try your daddy's cell phone," she said. "I have a feeling he thinks resisting me includes not making any phone calls."

She lay the baby on a blanket on Reagan's bed. "We wouldn't want to mess up this pretty quilt while I'm changing you, now, would we?"

Restless during the afternoon, she had washed a load of the baby's clothes and changing blankets, then a set of sheets from the linen closet. She had stripped the double bed and replaced those sheets with the fresh ones, along with the quilt she had found that would look perfect in Reagan's room.

This had to have been his quilt. She examined the fine, even stitching and the artfully arranged squares and rectangles of cloth. "Somebody put a lot of love into making this, Sean. And look at it—all sports equipment. Baseballs, bats, footballs, hockey sticks and more. I'll bet this was your daddy's favorite quilt when he was growing up."

Not that Reagan would ever tell her that. As she had confessed to Tina, he didn't want to tell her much of anything.

"Well, anyway, this will be yours one day, so we need to keep it nice." She smiled at him. "No problem. I've gotten pretty good with all the diapering and changing clothes and feeding and burping, haven't I?" She ruffled his hair. "I do believe your peach fuzz has grown some since you've been here. Must be all the healthy bottles I've been giving you."

He squirmed on the bed.

"You're very welcome. Glad you like them. Your

daddy likes my cooking…well, my reheating, too." She glanced at the bedside clock and was shocked to see it was past eight. "Where *is* that man, anyway?"

She was just about to give in and get her cell phone when she heard a door close downstairs, followed by heavy footsteps. For a moment, her hands stilled and her throat tightened.

When she could chance speaking normally, she murmured, "Well, guess what? Daddy's home."

The words triggered a funny feeling in her stomach.

She scooped the baby up from the bed and snuggled him against her. "And I guess we need to go face the lion in his den, huh?"

The house didn't have a den, but when she went halfway down the stairs, she found Reagan sitting in the living room. He had his head resting back against the couch, and in the lamplight she could see his eyes were heavy-lidded.

She continued down the stairs and into the room. "Hi. You're h-here." To her surprise, instead of his usual jeans, he wore a pair of khaki shorts. "You worked out on the ranch all day in those?"

"No. I was too filthy even to walk into the house in the clothes I'd worn. I had the shorts in the truck, so I stripped down and showered out in the barn."

Putting those words into pictures in her mind sent another kind of feeling to her stomach.

"What did you do that got you so dirty?" she asked, needing to distract herself. All she wanted to do was to climb up on that couch and curl up beside him.

He exhaled heavily and raised his head. Then he rested it against the couch again. "I had to clear out part of a stream that had gotten choked with weeds and silt. It was a slow job with only the shovel and small ax I carry in the truck, but the stream feeds into other ranches and provides some of the water for their herds."

"Well, that was very neighborly of you. But we rent equipment at the store that would have helped do the job a lot easier."

He shrugged. "I didn't mind the work."

You didn't mind staying away from the house.

She swallowed those words and said instead, "There's some rotisserie chicken and a salad from the L-G in the refrigerator."

"You didn't have to buy that."

"Just being neighborly."

"Well, thanks. Maybe later." He stifled a yawn. "The workout wore me out. And with not getting any sleep last night—" He stopped, and now his eyes were fully open.

"Sounds like the same kind of night I had," she said lightly. "Must have been something in the lasagna."

He cleared his throat. "Ally, about yesterday—"

She shook her head. "Yesterday's over. We don't need to talk about it. I understand perfectly."

"You do?"

"Of course. You spelled everything out plainly enough for an eight-year-old to follow. You and I together wouldn't work. The timing's just not right."

"I'm glad—"

"I have to feed the baby." Cradling Sean against her, she went quickly down the hallway to the kitchen.

She knew Reagan would come after her, but she needed time to get herself together. At that moment, she couldn't handle hearing any more reasons for his rejection. She had a feeling surface conversation was still all she would get from him right now.

I'm glad—what?

I'm glad there are no hard feelings.

I'm glad you're taking it so well.

I'm glad you're behaving like an adult about this.

She took a deep breath. She would not risk letting herself get upset or having her blood pressure go up or her hands shake. None of that would be good for Sean.

Reagan hadn't appeared yet.

"It's okay," she told the baby. "We're going to get your bottle ready. And when your daddy walks in, I'll be cooler than an ice-cream soda."

By the time Sean drained every drop of formula from his bottle, she did feel cooler. And calm and collected and steady again.

"You're my hungry, growing little boy, aren't you?" she cooed. As she patted his back, he brought up a couple of loud burps that left them both smiling.

When she held him close, he cuddled against her, one arm resting against her as if he were giving her a tiny hug. She kissed the top of his head and whispered, "Someday, Sean, I want a baby just like you."

And…and right now, that was as far as she dared to go.

Chapter Nine

Reagan awoke with a start. Both groggy and disoriented, he pushed aside the blanket covering him. He had no idea where the blanket had come from or how long he'd been out, but he somehow knew it hadn't been long enough. Considering he'd paced the floor all last night...

He remembered doing that. And he recalled confessing it to Ally, just before he'd crashed.

After shaking his head as if he could fling away the grogginess clouding his thoughts, he rolled himself upright on the couch.

Ally sat curled up in the big leather club chair, almost within reach, with his son resting against her.

His grogginess evaporated. He fought reactions even a long, cold shower couldn't cure, because they weren't physical. But they *were* reactions. Not that F-word. *Feelings.* He didn't do feelings. He especially didn't do feelings since he'd learned how much they could hurt.

Reactions, though, he had thought he could handle. He hadn't realized until now that they were worse. They could scare a man half to death.

"You're still here," he managed.

"You noticed." She smiled.

"Guess I zoned out. What time is it?"

"Almost eleven."

"Jeez." He scrubbed his face with his palm. "I didn't mean to keep you this long."

"You didn't. Sean had his bottle later than usual, so I brought him in here to sit with me, and we both got comfortable."

"You could have settled him in his crib and headed out," he said. "You've got a long drive home."

"It *is* a hike," she agreed. "I have to tell you, I really see some advantages to living in town."

"If it's too much of a hassle to drive out here—"

"No, it's not that. I just meant that when I'm at home, I've got the L-G and the department stores and Sugar-Pie's all so close by."

With no need to shop from the internet. He envisioned her showing off her stretchy dress to him, and he thought again of that cold shower. All of a sudden, it seemed exactly what he needed.

"And in town," she went on, "I've got other friends around me. I give one of them a call, and in minutes we're meeting at SugarPie's or the Cantina. I was just thinking you must have been lonely when you were growing up, living all the way out here without other kids from school nearby."

"No time to get lonely. There's always a lot to do on a ranch."

"But *you* didn't work on it."

"Yeah, I did." Suddenly, he wanted to explain his answer to Ally.

Maybe it was the late hour or the lack of sleep, or the fact that he hadn't meant to keep her here so long. Or maybe, and most likely, it was his…reactions. His reaction of guilt at knowing his parents had always intended him to take his place on this ranch, and he'd disappointed them. His reaction of guilt at knowing he'd let Ally down last night, too.

Maybe it was all of the above. But he settled on telling himself talking would help to distract him. Would take his mind off the fact that he wouldn't be getting that cold shower anytime soon.

"I spent a lot of hours working on this ranch," he told her. "My dad was at it from sunup to sundown, of course. But I pitched in whenever I wasn't at school or doing homework or involved in whatever sport was in season."

"Then what about your mama? Being out here alone all day while you two were working, she must have been lonely."

He shook his head. "You can't know a lot about ranches, Ally, or you'd know ranch wives keep as busy as anyone. Besides, my mom was friendly with lots of women who live out here. And others from town, too. I told you she knew Mrs. B from the community center, right?"

Ally nodded.

"She was friendly with your mom and Shay's Grandma Mo, too, and all the ladies in their women's circle, the knitting circle, the crafts club."

"She made the quilt that's upstairs, didn't she?" she asked softly. "The one with all the sports equipment on it."

"Yeah." That was one thing he didn't want to talk about. "Her groups met out here at the ranch sometimes."

"Yes, I remember coming here once with my mama."

He remembered her here, too, sitting on the corral fence and making him wonder if she'd never before seen a horse being groomed. Now he wondered something else. Had she had that crush on him even all the way back then?

He didn't dare bring that up. He couldn't risk mentioning anything that might give Ally some encouragement.

Last evening, he had told her the truth when he had said things couldn't work out between them.

And all last night, when he'd had such trouble sleeping, he'd reminded himself he sure wasn't going to parade a string of temporary women in front of his son.

"Well, anyway," he said, "my mom had plenty to do to keep her busy, yet she still had time for her friends and her clubs. I'm sure whoever buys the ranch will manage to do the same."

And that ought to be a good reminder to them both that he wouldn't be around here much longer.

IN REAGAN'S ROOM the next afternoon, Ally finished straightening the piles of Sean's one-piece jumpers and footed pajamas and tiny little undershirts. Babies sure did go through a lot of clothes in a day.

For a moment, she held a pair of pajamas close to her face and inhaled the soft, clean scent that reminded her of Sean. Cuddling him close to her for so long last night, she had finally acknowledged that the little baby had stolen a piece of her heart.

His daddy had long ago taken the rest of it.

She didn't want a baby *just like* Sean—she wanted Sean.

And Reagan.

How ironic. Barely a week ago, she had still been fooling herself about not planning to be a mama. Now she couldn't deny she wanted Reagan to love her and marry her and help her give Sean brothers and sisters.

She wanted them to be a family.

Somehow, she had to help Reagan leave the past behind. Otherwise, they would never have even the chance of a future together.

"You've got a fetish for pajamas?"

At the sound of his voice, she jumped.

Turning, she found him watching her from the doorway. "You're in early." She looked him over. He wore his khaki shorts again and a fresh T-shirt. "And you're all washed up."

He laughed. "Ally, that's not something you ever want to say to a man."

Her cheeks burned. "That's not what I meant, and you know it as well as I do. I'm only saying you must have showered outside again."

"I did. Now, back to that pajama fetish of yours."

She couldn't tell him the truth, that the scent of the laundry made her feel closer to his son. And to him. "I was just making sure they came through the wash okay," she said inanely.

"Have you checked out mine?"

"I haven't washed anything of yours—except the sheets—and you know *that* as well as I do, too." But she was willing—oh, so willing—to play the game. She tilted her head and batted her lashes. "So how can I possibly know if you even *wear* pajamas?"

He laughed. "I guess you couldn't know."

"Exactly." Smiling, she gathered up the clean laundry from the bed and walked to the dresser. Reagan stayed in the doorway, not threateningly, not pushing, just watching her and, she had to admit, giving her a thrill at the thought that she had his attention.

Now she just had to find a way to keep it.

She closed the dresser drawer. The quilt she had spread across the bed last night lay neatly folded on the chair beside the dresser. Frowning, she turned to Reagan. "I thought you liked that quilt. You didn't want to use it?"

For a moment, his eyes held an expression she couldn't read. An instant later, it was gone. "I was too hot," he said. "And it's too juvenile. I'm not a kid anymore."

"Neither am I," she shot back. That had certainly gotten his attention. He ran his gaze over her, leaving her skin heating everywhere he looked.

After taking a slow deep breath, she held out her hand.

Reagan sucked in a breath. He'd come upstairs looking for Ally only to let her know he was inside the house. But he wouldn't be honest if he didn't acknowledge— to himself, that is—the shot of adrenaline that had run through him when he'd found her alone in his bedroom. And he wouldn't be normal if he didn't accept the invitation she was offering.

Hell, he'd spent the day thinking about her, and there she stood, somehow looking both bold and shy at the same time. The combination made him want to do things he shouldn't even think about. But he'd turned her down the other night. How could he do that to her again?

He crossed the room. When he took her hand and she tightened her fingers around his in another invitation, he stopped resisting. He wrapped his free arm around her and took her mouth, too. It was firm and soft, molding to his. And so was she, nestling her body against his as if they'd been made to match. The thought of where else they would fit together had his heart thumping double time.

He couldn't have sworn which of them made the first move toward the bed, but he was glad to see she was as eager as he was to get there. He was determined to have the pleasure of seeing all of her.

Though he tried to take things slow, anticipation and eagerness spurred him on. One kiss led to five or six, and then to his hand on her blouse. Ally's murmur of pleasure gave him permission to do more.

The colors in the fabric seemed to blend together as he undid her buttons. The sight of pink lace beneath the blouse made his hand shake. She traced his knuckles with her fingertips as if guiding him, urging him on.

"Reagan," she murmured, "do you know how many times I've thought about us like this?"

He kissed her temple. "Not as many as I have lately."

"Oh, I doubt that." She laughed, low and sexy. His fingers fumbled on a button. "I've had a crush on you forever."

He kissed her cheek. "Forever, huh?"

"Oh, yes. Since third grade."

"That's a long time."

"Mmm-hmm. But I've always known this would happen someday. And I'm happy it finally has."

He smiled. "I'm hoping I can make you even happier."

"Oh, you will."

He ducked his head to kiss her jaw. Her curls brushed his face, teasing him.

"I've waited such a long time," she said, "just for you."

He stilled for a moment, then raised himself up on one elbow to look at her again. Her lips were moist, her eyes bright. Her hair fanned out, nearly covering his pillow. She was his for the taking, and she had waited...

"Just for me," he said.

She nodded.

"Are you...are you telling me you've never been with anyone?"

"No." She laughed, and her cheeks turned pink. "I mean, yes. You're right. That's what I'm telling you."

This time when he sucked in a breath, he nearly choked on it. "That's...that's special, Ally. You don't just sleep with someone for the first time and then walk away. And I *am* walking away. We talked about it last night." Regretfully, he pulled her shirt closed. "I'm not staying. You've known that since the beginning. And I won't take advantage of you."

She sat up. The shirt gaped open, giving him another glimpse of pink lace and soft, tanned curves. He looked away.

"You're not taking advantage of me. How can you be doing that when I've told you how long I've wanted you? I love you, Reagan. I have since third grade."

He stood and backed up a step, as if putting distance between them would erase her words. But that thought was about as foolish as what she had just said. "You don't love me. At that age, nobody knows what love is. You're basing your feelings on a schoolgirl crush."

"No, I'm not."

"You don't realize it but, yeah, you are. Our paths barely crossed when we were growing up. Until last week we hadn't seen each other in years. And last night, you told me you'd understood what I said about no relationships." He took a deep breath. "I'm not saying this is all on you. You held out your hand, and I took it. But I thought you'd decided just to have a good time while I was here."

"A *good time*?" She closed her eyes as if she couldn't look at him.

"Yeah. My mistake. I misunderstood. Obviously. And if I'd known you'd never—" He clamped his jaw shut to force himself to stop babbling.

Before she could open her eyes or he could say anything to make the situation worse, he turned and left the room. But he couldn't leave behind the thoughts that chased him down the hall.

All right, maybe he'd been wrong. Maybe this had nothing to do with Ally wanting a good time. Maybe this was about something else entirely.

He believed her when she said she hadn't been with anyone else. He believed *she* believed she loved him.

For all these years, she'd hung on to that crush. Had she also held on to another fantasy—that he'd be the first guy to make love with her?

Chapter Ten

"You're seeing me twice in less than twenty-four hours," Ally said to Tina. "This must be your lucky day." She could tell by the look on her friend's face that she knew it hadn't been *her* lucky day.

They were in the kitchen of Tina and Cole's apartment upstairs in the Hitching Post. "Let me go check on the kids," Tina said, "and then I'll make us a cup of tea."

Ally laughed. "You sound just like Mama and Paz. They think a good cup of tea can solve anything, too. I'm hoping you're all correct."

Tina left the room, and Ally took a seat at the table.

She blinked, fighting tears again. She had almost lost the battle to hold them back earlier—when Reagan had blindsided her with his assumption she was with him only to have a good time. Knowing he could believe that had stunned her so completely, she had barely closed her eyes in time to hold back a sudden rush of tears.

He must have been just as astonished to hear she had never slept with anyone. But she hadn't lied about that. Or about anything else.

After he had left the room, she had buttoned her blouse and straightened her hair. Then she'd taken a deep breath before heading downstairs to stay with the baby. She had expected to find Reagan in the kitchen, but Sean was alone. He slept soundly in his playpen in the same position she had left him in when she had gone to put his freshly washed clothes away.

To her surprise, she heard Reagan's footsteps overhead on the uncarpeted hall floor, then sounds of doors closing and drawers shutting and several solid thumps, as if he had been moving furniture.

Or been trying to burn off excess energy.

The rest of the afternoon and evening had passed very quietly, probably because they never saw each other again. At least, not until it was time for her to leave.

Tina returned to the kitchen, eyed her and went to heat the teakettle.

Ally plucked a couple of paper napkins from the holder on the table and waved with them. "I probably should have called first to see if you were free to talk. Should I fold one of these for Cole?"

"No. He went into town for a while. And the kids are sound asleep. We'll have plenty of time to chat with no interruptions. Not like this morning."

Even as they both laughed, remembering the busy women's center waiting room, Ally swallowed a sigh of relief. Nothing against Cole, but she certainly couldn't have the conversation she wanted to have with Tina in front of her husband—or anyone else.

Once Tina had finished making the tea, she brought both mugs to the table and took her seat.

And Ally, The Girl Most Likely, said, "Well, brace yourself for some news. I gave Reagan the shock of his life tonight. I told him my deep, dark secret—that I'm the oldest virgin in Cowboy Creek."

Tina shook her head, but she did laugh. Weakly. She also put a comforting hand on Ally's arm.

Ally blinked and attempted to smile.

"Honestly, Tina," she said, meaning it, "I never thought of it as keeping a secret, or making a big sacrifice, just as standing by a decision I'd made. Standing by Reagan." As long as he was there, she had never cared about anyone else. She had never had a boyfriend, never slept around. Then he had left for college, and she never saw him again.

She shrugged and pleated her napkin. "You know, *chica*, when we had no idea if he'd ever come back, I might have changed my mind. I might have slept with someone. Working at the store, I've certainly run across plenty of cowboys. We know some of them were eligible." She rolled her eyes. "And some of them just thought they were—or wanted me to think it. But let's face it, other than the guys in that category, unattached bachelors have been few and far between in Cowboy Creek. So I didn't deliberately *save* myself for Reagan."

But as she had told him, she had waited for him.

Waited and hoped.

"You never found anyone who measures up to him," Tina said quietly.

They exchanged a glance, and Ally nodded. Her best friend knew just what to say, just what to offer—sympathy and understanding—because she knew exactly how Ally felt. Tina had dealt with these feelings, too.

"Anyway," Ally said, "Reagan didn't take the V-word very calmly. Or the L-word, either, come to think of it."

"You told him that, too?"

"Oh, yes. I didn't hold anything back. And I have to

tell you, if nothing else good came of the conversation, at least it helped him open up to me a bit more. In fact, I think he said more to me at one time tonight than he has since he's been back."

That hadn't surprised her, really, after she had seen how much her admissions had shaken him. But later, it had startled her when he had come downstairs and made his abrupt announcement. He was in for the night and she might as well leave early.

Limiting her time at the ranch could be part of a plan to ease her out of a job—and out of his life. Or it could be his way of avoiding feelings he didn't know how to deal with.

"After hearing all my confessions at once, I'm sure he started talking out of sheer panic. But he *did* talk to me. And he wanted me. And I wanted him." Knowing she couldn't hold back from Tina, she admitted, "The one thing I didn't mention to him was the part about wanting wedding bells and babies."

Tina's eyes rounded. Her reaction wasn't an insult, just an indication of the size of this surprise.

"I know." Ally laughed. "Imagine that. Ally Martinez, wanting the walk down the aisle and the white picket fence and the patter of little feet around the house. Who will ever believe it? I can barely understand it myself. But seeing you with Emilia...and since I've been babysitting Sean... He's the sweetest little baby, Tina. After taking care of him...well...I guess it's been coming on gradually without me even being aware of it, but becoming a mama now seems like a pretty good idea."

"It's a *wonderful* idea." Tina smiled. "But you know, you're not fooling me. It didn't matter how often or how loudly you joked about kids not liking you and you not liking them, I could always see past that." She paused, frowning. "But what—"

"Don't even say it," Ally interrupted. "I know just what you're thinking. 'But what are the chances *Reagan* will ever come around?' Right?" When Tina nodded, she shrugged. "Honestly, I don't know. Maybe the odds would be enormous, if only he wasn't holding back because of whatever happened to him."

She looked down at her tea mug.

Again tonight, she had gone through the ritual of collecting her things, assuring herself she would be returning to the ranch, reassuring herself she would come back strong. Somehow, she had to find a way to do that. For Reagan's sake—and for her own.

"I think," she said slowly, "he will come around and open up with me. If we have enough time. But now I want something else, too."

Yes, she liked the idea of helping Reagan get comfortable with her. But even more, she liked the idea of what she had just told Tina. "One day, I do want to settle down, and that was as big a surprise to me as it was to you. Meanwhile, I think The Girl Most Likely needs to find out what else she can learn about herself.

"We were right this morning, *chica*. I like my bright colors and flashy jewelry and being a drama queen. Sometimes. But it couldn't hurt to try something different. Maybe for the chance to see how Reagan will react," she admitted. Then she added truthfully, "But right now, I'm curious about trying something different just for *me*."

REAGAN HADN'T SPENT much time in the Cantina in the summer between graduating high school and then leaving for college. Yet the minute he stepped foot inside the place again, he noted many things he could have described from memory. The long bar with its polished wood top and row of round, padded swivel stools. The mirror spanning the wall behind the bar, with rows of liquor bottles lined up and reflecting against the glass. The pool table in one corner and dance floor in another, with the jukebox in between, blasting out a country song.

He thought of the dances in the high school gym and the times he'd seen Ally here at the Cantina with one kid or another from school. She sure loved to dance.

He didn't want those thoughts or the images that came with them. If he had his choice, he wouldn't think of her at all.

Knowing the trip tonight would revive some memories, he couldn't say exactly what had brought him here.

It wasn't for the beer, since he was drinking club soda. He didn't intend to have alcohol, as he had just dropped Sean off at Mrs. B's and soon would be driving back home with him to the ranch. He was glad the woman had her evening free and was willing to watch his son for a couple of hours.

He hadn't come here for conversation. He had Sean to chat with at home, though he had to admit the baby wasn't much of a talker. Not like someone else he knew.

He wasn't here even for companionship. He'd had that at the ranch, too. But he'd given up the chance to have…a good time… To be with someone who would… someone who might…

Dang. Face it, already.

Sure, he was interested in Ally. Because he hadn't

had sex for way too long. That's what it was. That's *all* it was.

Maybe if he kept telling himself that, he'd eventually believe it.

Frowning down at his mug, he finally and reluctantly admitted it was thoughts like those that had driven him from the house. Had sent him looking for a distraction. Right now, he needed someone he knew to walk through the doors of the Cantina.

After what seemed like weeks, someone did.

Cole Slater raised his hand in greeting. After grabbing a beer at the bar, he headed toward Reagan's booth as if they had made plans to meet here. Reagan sighed in relief. If anybody could carry a conversation, it was Cole.

"Expecting someone?" the man asked.

Reagan had to swallow a laugh. "Nope." He shook his head and gestured with his soda mug at the empty half of the booth. "All yours."

"Good." Cole slid onto the bench seat. "Mitch is getting off duty soon and stopping in for a quick one."

He nodded. At the Hitching Post on Sunday, he had learned Mitch Weston, another of his friends from school, was now a deputy sheriff in Cowboy Creek and married to Jed's middle granddaughter, Andi.

"We didn't get to talk much at dinner the other afternoon," Cole said. "Family suppers are great—and when you get all Jed's gang together, it's a big family. And a long dining room table."

"Yeah, it was." And good luck or bad, he'd wound up sitting next to Ally.

"Expect a call from Jed about a barbecue at the ranch. Meanwhile, what's been going on with you?"

He filled Cole in about earning his degree in Houston, then making the move to San Antonio for the new job and finally returning to Cowboy Creek to get his folks' place ready to sell. "If I can find a buyer, that is. Jed's asking around, but I haven't had any takers yet."

"You're selling the place?" Cole sounded surprised. But then, he worked for Jed and probably wouldn't mind having a spread of his own. And like any good wrangler, he wouldn't understand how a man could willingly give up the chance to own land.

Reagan didn't understand how, tonight, he could have willingly passed up—

"First I heard of you putting your place on the market," Cole said.

He forced his thoughts back to the here and now. And his future. "Yeah? You interested?" Maybe he could cut a deal tonight and be on his way home with Sean tomorrow. Except that, even with the work he'd done this afternoon going through closets and boxes upstairs at the house, he hadn't made a dent in all the stuff his parents had stored there. To tell the truth, he hadn't worked with full concentration. His thoughts had kept drifting to…other things.

Besides, he didn't mind going through years of accumulated household stuff. It was what would come after that bothered him. He'd have to sort through his parents' personal belongings, items he couldn't just cart up and have hauled away. As little as he liked the idea, he would have to face all those memories.

Cole shook his head. "Thanks, but I'm not looking to move. I'm more than happy to be where I am now. And Tina and I finally have the apartment at the hotel all fixed up. You'll have to come by."

"If I'm still here." Something Cole had said finally hit him. He frowned. "You hadn't heard I was selling the ranch? Jed didn't say anything?"

"Not to me."

"Have you been away from Cowboy Creek?"

"Not lately."

The idea flashed through Reagan's head that Jed might not have said anything to anyone about the ranch being on the market. But what would the man have to gain by that? He pushed the thought away.

"Speaking of being gone," Cole said, "you left out a few items in your itinerary. Somewhere along the line, you managed to acquire a baby."

"Yeah."

Cole raised an eyebrow.

Cowboy Creek High wasn't that big. Though they'd been at different grade levels, he and Cole had shared some classes, played sports together and had always been friends in school. Close enough friends that Reagan knew if he said nothing, he could expect Cole to follow up with a question. "Ex-girlfriend," he explained. "Things didn't work out, and I got custody of my son."

"Any chance of a reunion? As I can attest, sometimes circumstances change. Or people do."

"Not in this situation."

Cole nodded. "I'm betting you mentioned some of this to Jed." He laughed. "He's probably got you next on his list."

"List?"

"To match you up with someone, the way he did with me and Tina…and Mitch and Andi…and the match-making successes go on."

He shook his head. "No thanks. Not interested. It'd

be a waste of his time. Besides, he knows I'm leaving soon."

"That won't stop Jed. I'll bet that's why he invited you and Wes Daniels to dinner on Sunday. And why Tina asked Ally." Shaking his head, he laughed again. "They're best friends, but they couldn't be more different. And I sure can't see Ally hooked up with either of you guys, considering she doesn't want anything to do with kids."

"She doesn't?"

"Nope. She's always been up front about that."

Cole took his empty mug and went to the bar for a refill.

Reagan frowned. Ally had sure been up front with him about some things. But what Cole had just said about her not liking kids...that didn't seem like the Ally he knew, the one who was taking such good care of his son.

He thought back to what Jed Garland had said to him on Sunday.

A boy always needs his mama.

Right now, Sean was too young to notice, but he'd soon grow old enough to realize he didn't have a mother.

He and his son had already lived through one woman deserting them. He wouldn't have his boy become attached to a string of women who wouldn't become part of his life. And that's what had started all his thinking, his talking, his *reacting* last night. He had woken up on the couch and seen Sean cuddling much too comfortably against Ally.

He took a swig of club soda and set his mug down so hard, he thought he'd cracked it. He wasn't going to fall for the woman just because she had won his son's affections. He wasn't going to fall for the woman at all.

Chapter Eleven

Ally took a seat at one of the little round tables in Sugar-Pie's and smiled at Tina. After her friend's tea and sympathy at the Hitching Post and her own announcement about wanting to learn something new about herself, they had looked at each other and said in one breath, "Shopping trip!"

Now she pleaded, "Don't let me go crazy over the desserts, *chica*, or I won't fit into my new clothes."

Layne arrived and took their order, then eyed the department store bags Ally had left on an extra chair. "Looks like somebody went a little wild tonight."

Ally laughed. "No, just the opposite, actually." When Layne went back to the kitchen, Ally turned to Tina. "No flowers, no flounces, no bright colors. It's a good thing I didn't wear any of those clothes home from the store. Mama and Papa wouldn't have recognized me when I walked in the door."

"You know that's not true. And everything you bought looked great on you, especially that green shirt, the way it brings out your eyes."

"I need it to bring out more than that. I need to find a whole new personality."

"No, you don't. Just try being yourself when you're

around Reagan. You're wonderful just the way you are, and he'll see that, too."

"Thanks, *chica*." She could always trust her best friend forever to say something to cheer her up. "I hope I knock his socks off, as Jed would put it. But I was talking about myself again."

"What do you mean?"

She shrugged. "I may have won The Girl Most Likely award in high school, but you and I both know I've been playing that role since third grade. It's like a…well, I was going to say, like a mask, but that doesn't describe it well enough." She gestured to the sacks. "It's more like all these new clothes I bought tonight. I put on my role as easily as I get up and get dressed in the morning. And then at night I go home and take it off with the rest of my clothes. I've done that for so long, I don't even know who I really am any more.

"We were right this morning, Tina. It couldn't hurt to try something different. If Reagan likes that someone else, great. If he doesn't…well, I can't worry about that right now. After all these years, I think it's more important to try something different for *me*."

"Then, Reagan or no Reagan," Tina said, "this is the perfect chance."

"I think so. And the clothes are just the beginning."

"That's for sure." Tina laughed. "Our stop at the drugstore was a trip down memory lane, wasn't it?"

"It was." Ally reached for that smaller sack and set the two items she took from it onto the table. "Look at this. Light pink blush and clear lip gloss and that's it. My face will be more naked than the day I was born."

Even as Tina laughed, she shook her head. "Stop, Ally."

"Okay. But after all, this is the same look I wore in

junior high. Actually, as attached as I am to my makeup case, I have to say I think I'm going to like the change."

"Permanently?"

"Hey, let's not get crazy. When I go out to party at the Cantina with the girls, I'll still need to play the role." She winked. "After all, I owe it to everyone who voted to give me that award."

"I'M RUNNING LATE," Ally announced as she entered the kitchen at home the next morning.

Mama stood at the sink. Papa already sat at the table, eating breakfast.

She glanced at the clock on the stove. How she could possibly be late when it had taken a half minute to do her makeup this morning, she didn't know. Maybe it had something to do with all the daydreaming she had done in the shower...

"I shouldn't have stayed out so late last night at Sugar-Pie's."

"And then a call from Tina?" Mama asked with her back still to Ally. "You waited for her to let you know she got home all right?"

"Of course." They always checked in with each other on nights Ally drove back to town from the Hitching Post or Tina returned home, although Tina, especially, was used to driving on the long, dark stretches of road.

Ally wondered if she would ever have a need to get used to that.

Right now, though, she needed to focus on getting to work. "I'm just going to drop a slice of bread into the toaster and eat it on the run."

Her mother turned from the sink, ready to protest, Ally knew. Instead, she looked her up and down. "What's this, *querida*?"

"It's the new me," she said, holding her hands up and twirling slowly, the way she had done when she'd shown off her dress to Sean. "Do you like it?"

"What's wrong with the regular you?" Papa demanded.

"Hush," Mama said. "Every girl likes a change once in a while. You look very nice in that shirt and slacks. Although very different without any jewelry... Well, sit. Your eggs have been keeping hot on the stove. And if you show up ten minutes late, it would be the first time in all the years you've worked there. They won't fire you."

"That is true. I'm nothing if not dependable, right?" She wished for the first time in those five years that she could play hooky from the day job. She would much rather be working her second job out at the ranch with Sean. And Reagan.

As if Mama had read her mind, she asked, "And how was Sean yesterday? I saw Nan at the club meeting last night, and she said he was a bit fussy with his bottle."

"He was fine when I was there." She recalled how he had reached out to her. Of course, she knew he was too little to give her a hug, but still, her throat tightened at the memory. Maybe someday...if he were still here...

Mama left the kitchen, and Ally carried her plate to the table.

Papa took his turn to look her over. "I would ask if you're getting yourself all dolled up for some boy, but I guess that doesn't apply since you're all dolled down."

She laughed and kissed the top of his head. "No, not for some boy. Not for some man, either. This new look is for me." And to her surprise, just as she had said to Tina last night, she liked it.

She had restrained her wild curls and put on her minimal makeup and worn the blouse Tina had said brought out her eyes. It was a totally different look, but one she could easily see herself wearing again and again. She looked down at her bare arm and frowned. Mama had noticed the missing bracelets right away, and she had to admit her arm felt bare without them.

One bangle bracelet…or maybe two…wouldn't have hurt.

Mama returned to the kitchen carrying a long white box. "Ally, I have just the thing for your new look." She removed the lid and held out the box.

After one glance at the delicate gold chain that had belonged to her beloved *abuela*, Ally let out a gasp of pleasure. Then she immediately shook her head. "That's your favorite bracelet, Mama! I can't wear that to the store. What if I broke it?"

"You can keep it in your locker until you finish work." Mama covered the box again and set it on the counter beside Ally's shoulder bag.

"All right," she agreed. "I can do that. Thanks."

She glanced again at the covered box. Not that she was the least bit superstitious, but…

She sincerely hoped the family heirloom would bring her good luck.

FIGHTING SOME UNEASINESS, Reagan left his bedroom and went down the stairs. He had heard Ally arrive at the house a short while ago.

The brief time that had passed between the sounds of her car door closing and her footsteps going back and forth in the kitchen had told him she'd gone directly inside. She couldn't have known he wasn't in the barn, as usual. Normally, she stopped by there first to give him a chance to see his son.

This change in her routine had to be a sign she was still upset about what had happened—and hadn't happened—between them yesterday.

He needed to man up and get any awkwardness about that over with.

As he strode along the downstairs hall, he made sure his boots hit hard against the wooden floor. He didn't want to startle her.

The only sound he heard from the kitchen was the splash of running water. No radio playing. No Ally humming along to the music or talking to Sean.

She stood at the sink, faced away from him. Her hair hung in one long braid down her back, the curls tamed at the top by a silver clip and at the bottom by a ribbon tied in a small bow. First time he'd seen it that way since grade school.

He smiled, imagining her surprise if he tugged on the ribbon.

Not gonna happen. Nothing was going to happen between them. At the reminder, he curled his fingers into a fist.

She shut off the faucet and moved over to set something on the counter.

With the water running, she probably hadn't heard his boots. He cleared his throat.

She turned, saw him and gave him a brief smile. Cool, impersonal. Nothing like he'd gotten used to seeing. "Hi. I didn't know you were in the house. Sean's asleep. I was going to bring him to see you a bit later.

I just wanted to take care of this." She gestured to the counter and stepped aside.

Recalling what happened the night they'd stood together at this counter after dinner made him cautious. He moved forward but not too close.

She had been watering a small plant with dark purple blooms and plain green leaves. A big difference from the vase of colorful, long-stemmed flowers she'd had on the table that night. He had left the vase on the counter where she'd put it after straightening up the kitchen, but by the next afternoon, the flowers had disappeared.

"We're having a plant sale at the store," she said, "so I brought one for the windowsill here. I gave it water, since it was looking a little blah. That's probably why it was on sale." Another brief smile. "I don't want to keep you if you're headed to the barn. As I said, I'll be here with Sean."

"Right." She was different today, and it wasn't just the tied-back hair or her plain green blouse, nearly the same shade as the plant's leaves. There was no big smile. No quick, cute chatter. No laugh.

He knew why. But as much as he regretted not being with her the way she'd wanted him to be…the way he'd wanted, too…he knew he had done the right thing by turning her down. No matter how much he might like what she was offering, he'd told her the truth. He wasn't about to take advantage of her. And considering how little time he'd be here, their getting together wouldn't amount to more than a one-night stand.

"I'll be working inside this afternoon. Upstairs," he clarified quickly.

She nodded and plucked a withered bloom from the plant. "That's fine."

He frowned. She seemed to be dealing with this awkward situation better than he had expected. Better than he was handling it. He had to say something else, or she would think he was the one who hadn't gotten over what had happened. "You'll need to take that plant home once I leave."

"Provided it's still alive. I'll do my best, but I don't have much of a green thumb."

No grin. No laugh. No way to tell if she'd been joking or not. A stupid thing to get hung up on, but she'd never before been so hard to read. He liked the braid and the blouse just as much he liked what she normally wore. But he missed the laughing, bubbly Ally. It was that lack of chatter that really had him wondering. "Are you okay?"

"Me?" She sounded surprised. "I'm fine. Why?"

"You seem…quiet."

Now she gave a little laugh. "I do have quiet moments once in a while. You just haven't seen too many of them."

He nodded, not knowing where to go with that. But she did seem more like herself now. He gestured across the room. "There might be some plant food still in the utility closet. I'd seen a good collection of pots in there the other day."

She glanced at him. "Your mama grew houseplants?"

He nodded. "All kinds, but ones like that, especially." He hadn't recalled that till now. Or maybe he hadn't wanted to remember.

"Violets use a different type of food. I've seen it at the store. If you don't find any in the closet, I'll pick some up tomorrow. I'm sure this plant could use some extra nurturing."

Like the extra cuddling she'd been giving his son.

He backed a step, then stopped.

With him planning to work upstairs, she'd be down here alone with Sean all afternoon. Again. Lots more time for Sean to get too close to her. The thought bothered him as much now as it had last night at the Cantina.

Before he could second-guess himself, he said, "I'll be sorting out some things upstairs, trying to figure out what to toss and what to donate. Maybe you could give me a hand."

She shrugged. "Sure."

"Good. But first, I'll check on that plant food."

Halfway to the utility closet, he almost stumbled, realizing suddenly the mistake he had made. Sure, he had solved his problem of her staying alone with Sean all afternoon.

But he'd also made it certain she would be spending that time with *him*.

The rush of pleasure following that thought warned him of trouble ahead.

Chapter Twelve

In the extra bedroom upstairs in the ranch house, Ally knelt on the floor and eyed Reagan. She wasn't sure what had made him ask her to help him today. A little change in clothing and makeup couldn't have caused *this* much of a turnaround.

Besides, as she had realized on the ride to the ranch this afternoon, it wasn't her clothes or her hair or anything else that would make Reagan willing to talk. He had to come to that decision on his own. And for his sake, she wanted that most of all.

She took his request for help as a step in the right direction. An indication he was getting more comfortable around her.

One step at a time suited her just fine.

They were spending the afternoon in a spare bedroom on the second floor, which his mama had evidently used for storage. They hadn't tackled the closet or the drawers of the dresser yet but were slowly working their way through the boxes that had been piled throughout the room.

"This one is extra towels and washcloths," she reported as she investigated yet another box.

Reagan opened the flaps of a large carton, and they both backed away from the scent of mothballs.

"Mostly out-of-season clothes, I'd guess," he said. "My mom used to swap out the clothes from our bedrooms a couple of times a year." He rose abruptly and carried the box over to set it next to the doorway, where they had stacked cartons they had already sorted through.

Out-of-season clothes and houseplants. Two such simple subjects. But talking about both meant progress for Reagan.

Across the room, he was still emptying and sorting through the contents of the carton. With his back to her, she had the opportunity to look him over.

In grade school and junior high, she'd been caught up mostly in his crooked smile and the dark hair tumbling over his forehead. By high school, she'd grown up some and widened her range of interest.

Now, she saw even more to like, from the dark hair clipped short against his tanned neck to his broad shoulders and tapering waist. She'd had plenty of chances to get an eyeful of Reagan in a football or basketball or track jersey. She had liked her chances even better during swim season, when nothing but chlorinated pool water blocked her sight of his muscular chest and abs.

Feeling her cheeks heating at the visions so clear in her mind, she fanned her face and turned reluctantly back to work. She needed something besides a carton of hand towels to distract her.

She reached for the next small box and opened the flaps. "It looks like your mama liked to swap out more than just clothes. This carton has small appliances and utensils. Mostly duplicates, since I've already seen others downstairs. A can opener, a hand mixer and a few brand-new whisks and spatulas, still in the original packaging."

"Yeah, Mom always liked to have extras of all those things on hand. 'Emergency backups,' she used to call them. In a way," he said slowly, "you were right when you said what you did about us living out here, so far from town. Not that Mom ever felt lonely—or at least, if she did, I never heard about it. But she did sometimes feel cut off from all those stores you love living close to. Especially the grocery store."

Glancing up, she said, "Mrs. Browley told me your mama was an excellent cook."

"She was." One side of his mouth curved the slightest bit, as if he wouldn't risk a full smile. "That's why she always had her emergency backups. She couldn't just make a quick trip to the L-G to pick up a new can opener or an extra quart of milk. She made almost everything from scratch, and if an appliance broke or we ran short of an ingredient she needed to make supper, she didn't want to worry about being caught without."

"I can understand that," she said. "Though I'll admit if it were me, I would miss shopping for clothes and shoes more than I would the kitchen stuff. I'm not much of a cook. And speaking of cooking…" She hesitated, then admitted, "That lasagna we had the other night… it was the first time I'd made it. And it was mostly put together with assistance from *my* mama. I don't really know how to cook anything much more complicated than eggs and bacon or home fries and ham steak."

"Everybody has to start somewhere," he said.

She smiled. "Yes, they do." That was true whether

it came to learning how to cook or letting down your guard to trust someone.

He gestured to the boxes they had piled in a stack for donations. "I'm going to take these cartons out and put them in the back of the truck."

He left with his arms full, and she watched until he had disappeared from her sight.

As much as she would like to attribute his sudden chattiness to her uncharacteristic lack of chatter, she knew better. His conversation most likely came from feelings stirred up by their job in this room, feelings he refused to acknowledge.

From as far back as she could remember, her parents had always encouraged her to say whatever she felt, to talk about everything that went on in her day, good and bad. When she was done, they shared with her. And when the three of them got together with her aunts and uncles and cousins, it was always more of the same—usually announced in front of the entire family.

Someone like Reagan, who talked so little about himself, his past and his life in general, would probably need much more encouragement before he would share his feelings, even in a private conversation.

There was so much she wanted to ask him. She knew about his mama's illness and that she had passed away just a few years ago. She'd never known why he hadn't come back after that to see his father. But this wasn't the time to ask about those things, either. Reagan had finally made the attempt to talk. She couldn't risk having him shut down again.

She stood and went over to one corner of the room.

They had left Sean asleep in his infant seat. He was now awake, his blue eyes open wide, his gaze scanning the room. She didn't know how far babies his age could see, but she knew by the way his gaze fastened on her that he saw her approaching him.

"Hey, baby," she said. "It's Ally. Remember me?" Her braid had fallen forward over her shoulder while she was bending down sorting through the cartons. She lifted the end of the braid and waved it at Sean. "This is the new me. But don't let the plain hair and clothes fool you. I'm still the same Ally on the inside."

Which was, of course, nothing but the truth.

"And you know what? I think your daddy might like the new me *and* the old me."

But she wanted more than *like*.

No matter what Reagan said about her schoolgirl crush, she genuinely loved him. And she truly believed he could learn to love her, too.

ALL DAY, REAGAN had kept one eye on the clock, waiting for the time he'd get to see Ally again.

He didn't know why she had made the changes she had the day before. Though he liked her sweet, quiet side as well as he liked the flirty one, he missed the color and brightness and bubbliness of her. And he definitely missed the teasing. He hadn't realized how many times she had made him laugh since he'd been back.

He glanced from the corner of his eye to where she sat on one end of the couch. In the light from the lamp, she seemed fully focused as she dug through a box she had brought down from the bedroom this afternoon. Having her this close to him made him want her even closer.

He rubbed his eyes as if he could erase her image from them.

"Tired?" she asked.

"No." But he was—tired of wanting her yet needing to keep away.

The room went quiet again. Her silence was getting to him, and he wasn't used to having to carry the conversational ball. "Maybe we should stop for the night. It *is* getting late. And after all, it's Friday."

Just one short week since he'd come into the house and found her in the living room dancing while she dusted. One very long week since he'd finally acknowledged he'd been thinking about asking her out. Even then he'd decided that had been a crazy idea. Yet only a few days later, he'd given in to her invitation and they had wound up in bed together.

But not for long. He'd found his common sense before he could give in and make a huge mistake. He had to be grateful for that.

She hadn't spoken, and he tried again. "I imagine you have plans."

She shook her head. "This sounds like the conversation we had last week. And no, I don't have anything special going on tonight, either. Or tomorrow. I can come and spend the day. We've barely made a dent in sorting through those boxes upstairs."

His mind yelled no, but too late. His head was already nodding. It wasn't so much that he needed help but that he wanted the chance to be with her. How had he gone from cutting down the time she spent alone with Sean to this?

She gave him her brilliant smile and went back to riffling through the box, leaving him struggling for something else to say. With relief, he heard her give a little "ah" of satisfaction as she pulled a book from the box she'd been pawing through.

"Look what I found," she said. "Your senior yearbook."

He stared at it. "No big deal. Everybody's got the same edition." Cowboy Creek High School was so small that technically they didn't have yearbooks, only school annuals covering all four grades every year. "You've got a copy of this one on a shelf at home somewhere."

"Yes, but I always love looking through them. Come on, let's take a peek."

For a moment, the bubbly side of Ally's personality resurfaced. Her voice had filled with enthusiasm. Her eyes sparkled.

She edged closer to him and sat back, and he caught the subtle scent of spice.

He fisted his hands on his knees and focused on the annual.

She paged through the pictures of the principals and teachers, the yearbook staff, the highlights of the school plays and fund-raiser fairs. When she got to the group photos of clubs and teams, she turned the pages more slowly.

"You must have enjoyed high school," she said.

"I did."

"How about college?"

"Fair enough. How about you? High school must have been fun. You don't get an award like you did without being the life of the party, at least sometimes."

"Oh, I am that," she assured him, flashing another smile. "And I had a great time all through school. I haven't missed a reunion yet, either." Like the annuals, the reunions included anyone who had graduated from the school. "You'll have to come back for one someday."

"Someday," he echoed. He thought she might push the point, but instead she returned her attention to the book she held.

As she began to turn another page, he reached down to stop her. Her hand was warm and soft and made him recall the flirty Ally reaching out to him. He pulled his hand back.

"Wait," he said, indicating a photo, a group of girls in bathing suits at the community pool. "That's you, isn't it?" He knew it was. He studied her picture. All through school, she'd had longer, curlier, darker hair than most of the other girls. And in this photo, even as a sophomore, she definitely had more curves.

Why had he never noticed that back then?

He glanced up and saw her cheeks had turned pink. He smiled. No matter how she acted, quiet or flirty, she was two halves of the same whole. The same Ally.

And he liked them both. Too much.

She snapped the yearbook closed. "We should put this up in your room with all your other school stuff." She stood and walked over to stand by the stairs, as if she planned to do just that.

"What does it matter?" he asked. "I'll be packing up everything in that room soon, including the yearbooks, and getting rid of most of it."

She gasped. "Getting rid of it? Reagan, you can't. All those keepsakes. All your memories."

"Maybe I don't want the memories," he said before he could think twice.

No matter which Ally she chose to be, that's what she did to him.

"You just said you enjoyed high school." She stood hugging the book as if she could hold the memories inside it for him. The same way she held his son. "Maybe," she said softly, "it's the memories that came after these that you don't want to keep."

He clamped his jaw tight and looked away.

"Talk to me," she said. "Tell me about Sean."

The little hitch in her voice did him in. So did the fact that she'd asked about his son.

Not "Sean's mother." Not "your ex." She wanted to know about the baby. And as much as it had bothered him that his son was getting too attached to her, he wanted to tell her.

Maybe because he'd never told anyone the full story.

Maybe because he knew he wouldn't be here much longer. He could get it out and walk away.

In any case, he took a deep breath, locked his hands on his knees and looked back at her. "The sixty-second version. I met Elaine in college. We dated, got serious. She said she loved me, I told her the same thing. I planned to propose, but before I got that far, we discovered Sean was coming along. He wasn't part of her plans. And then neither was I."

Even from across the room, he could see her eyes fill with tears. "She didn't want your baby?"

"She didn't want anybody's baby."

"And so...so you broke up with her?"

He shook his head. "No. When I said 'neither was I,' I meant that was her decision. As it turned out, she was looking for fun in the short-term. She didn't want a husband or a family." He stared down at his clenched hands on his knees, had to flex his fingers to loosen them. This was turning into more than a sixty-second explanation, but now that he'd started, he couldn't seem to stop.

"Then..." She paused.

He knew what was coming. "Then how do I have Sean?" He shrugged. But he had to blink a time or two before he could continue, and he couldn't keep his fingers from curling into fists. "She didn't want my baby. I did. I made arrangements to take care of her medical expenses until Sean was born. I didn't force her into it. I made the offer. I told her it was her body, her choice. She made that decision, too."

For a moment, he struggled to fight all the pain he'd felt at the time, suddenly coming at him again now in spades. "Yeah," he admitted. "You were right. Those are sure some memories I don't want to keep."

He went to take the annual from her. "I'll put this up in the room." Her eyes were still teary, but she gave him a shaky smile. He tried not to wince. She thought he had agreed about saving the book. Saving the good memories, at least.

Now he was the one clutching the annual, using his grip on it to keep from reaching for her.

He moved past her and up the stairs, knowing what she couldn't know—he'd been avoiding other memories for a longer time, since his senior year in high school. He was still trying to run from them, the way he had just run from her.

She would be harder to escape.

Whichever Ally she decided to be at any moment didn't matter to him. Either one...both... He wanted her. And he knew she wanted him.

It all came down to sex.

The changes that had happened in his life because of his ex.

The reason he couldn't keep from wanting Ally. But even if she came to him with another offer, he now had another reason for turning her down.

He didn't think he could sleep with her once and walk away.

Chapter Thirteen

As it turned out, Ally didn't stay much later at Reagan's.

Instead, she had spent a very long night awake and alone, replaying everything he had told her.

After hearing his voice crack more than once, after seeing him blink to ward off what had to be tears, after seeing his shoulders hunch and jaw tighten and his fists clench as he'd shared that story, she hadn't been able to close her eyes all night.

She would be the first to admit she hadn't thought she wanted children. But Reagan's baby? How could that woman not have wanted Reagan's child? How could she just have thrown Reagan and Sean away?

On her long drive out to the ranch in midmorning, those questions kept ringing in her head.

Those questions, and something else Reagan had shared.

She said she loved me, I told her the same thing.

And still he and Sean had been deserted.

No wonder he refused to believe her when she told him she had loved him for so long.

She closed her car door and took a deep breath, then started toward the house. She had arrived around the time she had last Saturday, and again she had brought a sack of sweet rolls from SugarPie's. Doing something twice didn't make it a routine, but the repetition of her actions this morning, the normalcy of them, helped right her world, a world that had gotten shifted off course last night by hearing Reagan tell his story.

She could only imagine what living it had done to him.

She set the sack of sweet rolls on the counter. From it came the scent of yeasty, cinnamony goodness, and that helped to right her world a little, too.

Everyone needed a little sweetness in life.

She left the sack on the kitchen counter, checked that her braid was tied with its ribbon and her plain blouse tucked in and neat.

Face it, she was using these delaying tactics because she was nervous about seeing Reagan this morning. Nervous about how he would feel after having said so much about himself when that wasn't his way. Nervous about how he would feel now that she knew.

After taking a deep breath and forcing a smiling, she went into the living room. From the bottom of the stairs, she called his name.

"We're up in my room," he called back.

She found him changing Sean. "Good morning," she said. "How's…" …*my little boy today?* she had begun to ask the baby. She caught herself just in time and focused on Reagan. "How's everything going?"

"Fine so far. We've just finished breakfast." He looked from her to Sean. "Haven't we, little man?"

Hearing the love in his voice made her heart melt. He was such a good daddy. Sean was such a good baby.

She wanted them both to be hers.

As if reacting to his daddy's voice, Sean flailed his arms.

She and Reagan laughed. It was all so normal.

Except that, to her ears, her laugh sounded shaky. Not surprising, since it matched the rest of her right now. A good kind of shakiness that came from feeling happy. Excited. Hopeful.

Reagan had shared something of himself with her, and he wasn't backing away.

She took a seat on the edge of the bed. To her surprise, the quilt she had last seen on the dresser was now spread neatly across the mattress. She ran her hand along the surface.

Reagan must have noticed her movement. He said, "Sean likes it."

"I'm sure he does. I told him someday you'd be teaching him about all these sports."

"I sure will."

His smile made her as happy as the sound of his voice had made Sean. She felt a sudden urge to wave her arms a bit, too. Resisting the impulse, she looked down at the quilt again. She recalled asking Reagan about it once before and how abruptly he had answered the question. *Yes, his mama had made it. Change of subject.*

Now the silence that had fallen between them felt relaxed. Comfortable. That, and the fact that he'd talked so naturally to her this morning, prodded her to bring up the subject again. "My mama makes quilts like this. With her crafts club. Your mama hand made this one for you, didn't she?"

He nodded. "Yeah. As I'd said, she was in that club, too."

"I know. And it looks like your father was pretty handy, himself." She touched the headboard of the bed. Carved across the surface of the wood was a single row of alternating Stetsons and horseshoes. The carving matched those on the top drawers of the nightstand and dresser. "I'll bet he made this entire set."

A new silence hung on, not quite as comfortable.

"Yeah," he said finally. "My dad was always good at working with wood."

She gestured across the room. "The shelves in here. The bookcases and cupboards downstairs in the living room. He built those, too." It wasn't a question.

"Yeah. A long time ago."

"You can take the bedroom set with you, but what about the rest? If it were mine, it would break my heart to walk away."

He shrugged. His eyes looked bleak. "Sometimes that's the best thing to do with memories."

"You said that last night about your yearbooks and school keepsakes. And now, you want to walk off from all these things your parents made, just for you? Why, Reagan?" she asked softly.

The flirty side of her might not have asked. But every part of her wanted to know his reasons.

He had been a happy kid in grade school and junior high, a good student, eventually a town hero after he'd excelled on the high school teams. She had never heard of him getting into any trouble, drinking and driving, pulling stupid pranks or hanging out with the wrong crowd.

The quiet side of her said to let this go. But again, every part of her had its own ideas.

She would bet Reagan had never allowed himself to tell anyone what he had told her—and she was certain there was something else bothering him. His story last night was heart-wrenching, yet he *had* shared it. How bad could his other memories be that he refused even to mention them?

She wanted to do more for him than sorting boxes and even minding his son. She wanted to help him with everything that was haunting him, even if all he would let her do was to listen as he talked.

"There are more memories, aren't there?" she asked. "More that you want to walk away from?"

For a long moment, he looked across the room at the shelves and the trophies and the bulletin board with the picture of himself and his parents on vacation. She could almost see the thoughts whirling in his head.

Should I tell her? Should I trust her? Should I keep it to myself the way I've always done?

She pressed her hands together in her lap and waited.

Sean squirmed on the bed, turning his head as if trying to find her. She leaned forward to touch his hand.

On the dresser, Reagan's cell phone rang. He hesitated, and she told herself he wouldn't answer it. He didn't want the interruption. He planned to talk to her, to answer her question.

After another ring, he turned and went to the dresser. "Hey, Jed," he said. "Nothing much at all."

And she could almost swear to knowing what Jed Garland had said.

What's going on?

And what *was* going on? A conversation she had hoped would bring Reagan a few steps closer. A conversation that might have just ended for now.

Swallowing a sigh, she lifted Sean from the bed.

REAGAN PARKED THE pickup truck under the same shade tree he'd found last Sunday. Today, he and his son had company. Ally had come along with them to the Hitching Post—at Jed Garland's invitation.

This trip, it was Ally who took care of transferring Sean to his infant seat. He watched her movements, quick and steady, and thought about what Cole had told him about her not wanting anything to do with kids. Sure couldn't prove it by looking at her.

How many sides of her were there, anyway?

He wouldn't be around long enough to find out.

That was partly why he'd been relieved to get the saved-by-the-bell call from Jed. There were many things he could have told Ally in answer to her questions, but what was the point when he was leaving soon?

"I'll take that little boy from you," he said, reaching for the carrier. For a moment, they both gripped the seat's handle. His fingers brushed Ally's, and he had a picture of them walking across the yard, hand in hand, linked by the baby. Looking like a family.

She let go of the carrier and walked beside him and Sean.

He wasn't sure why he'd agreed to come here for the barbecue with her.

He wasn't sure why he'd done anything lately. At first, he had told himself he was spending more time with her because he'd wanted to put some space between her and Sean. Then he told himself he had to be with her to see how she was taking care of his son. And now, he'd fallen back on the excuse of needing help clearing out the house.

He was almost as good at telling himself stories as she was at spinning them for herself.

"There's Jed," she said, pointing to one side of the

yard. "They've probably already got the fire going. It was nice of him to invite us to the barbecue."

"It was," he agreed. "Though maybe my time would be better spent working at the house."

"Everybody needs a little relaxation sometime. We can get back to sorting things out tomorrow."

She said it so readily, so easily, as if they *were* a family. Or at least, a couple.

The longer he let her stay around, the more people saw them together, the more she would hang tight to her fantasy that she was in love with him.

As tightly as she had gripped his son's carrier, keeping him safe.

As tightly as she had wrapped her arms around the school annual, holding his memories.

He needed to wrap up his business here and get back to San Antonio. Back to work. The phone call with his boss the other day had included a few complaints about being shorthanded. Besides, his stockpile of vacation hours was running low, and he'd never know when he might need that time for Sean.

Jed saw them coming and loped across the yard to greet them. He clapped a hand on Reagan's shoulder. "Glad you could all make it."

The older man turned to Ally. "You can head on inside if you like, take the baby out of this sun for now. The women can use a hand in the kitchen."

She laughed. "Paz must have left town, then. She knows better than to let me anywhere near her domain. I'm a disaster in the kitchen, remember?"

"You made a good meal yesterday," Reagan said, then clamped his jaw tight. He had enjoyed the supper, but he didn't need to encourage Ally. Or to broadcast the fact that they were spending time together that didn't involve her babysitting for Sean.

"Thanks. I'll take the baby," she said, reaching for the carrier again.

And again, he held on long enough to make sure she had a good grip. Then he watched her walk away with his son.

"Come sit for a while," Jed said. "We're only just building the fire, so it won't be too hot over there yet."

Standing right here, watching Ally walk away had gotten him hot enough. *Jeez.* He was salivating over the woman right in front of Jed, who, to hear Cole tell it, was New Mexico's biggest matchmaker. That's all he would need, to give the man an idea he was ready and willing to get hitched.

It would be a cold July in Cowboy Creek before he'd try that again.

He fell into step beside Jed.

"So Ally's doing some cooking out at the ranch, huh?" Jed asked.

He should've known the old man would pick up on his slip. "Sausage and eggs. Standard breakfast. For *supper*," he clarified hastily. "She made it at suppertime."

"I see." Jed smiled.

He'd bet Jed had seen and imagined and already turned the event into much more than it was. Just as Ally had probably done.

He glanced across the yard. Halfway to the back porch of the Hitching Post, she had stopped to talk to one of Jed's cowhands. Or the hand had stopped to talk with her.

He frowned. Not that he cared how Ally passed her time. But couldn't the guy see she was carrying Sean?

What man would hit up a woman holding another man's baby?

"That's a girl with a good heart," Jed said. "Loyal, too. They don't make them much better than Ally Martinez."

Which Ally? he wanted to ask. Did everyone out here at the Hitching Post know both sides?

Again, he wondered how many other sides there were to her, how many facets he hadn't yet seen. How much he had missed by turning down her invitation.

How many reasons she'd come up with to convince herself she loved him.

The thought brought him to a halt. Jed, oblivious to the fact that he had lost his companion, continued walking and joined a group of what looked like hotel guests.

From across the yard, Cole Slater raised a hand, hailing him. The other man held up a beer bottle and pointed to the cooler at his feet.

Reagan nodded and headed in that direction. His gaze strayed toward the hotel. Ally and the cowhand seemed to have plenty to talk about. He said something, and she laughed and swept her braid back over her shoulder.

Reagan envisioned her reaching out her hand to him.

He ground his teeth together, shifted his Stetson and wiped his brow. With a nod of thanks, he took the bottle Cole handled to him. "Just one," he said. "I'm driving. But a cold one will go down good right now. The temperature must have jumped a few degrees in the past few minutes."

"Could be," Cole agreed. "The sun's been strong, and we haven't had a cloud in the sky this afternoon."

"Yeah," he agreed—though he knew darned well it

wasn't the summer heat that had made him break out in a sweat.

His reaction had come from the memory of Ally's declaration of love. A declaration he hadn't believed, as he had made very clear to her. He'd laid out a valid argument then. He stood by his reasoning now.

They'd barely been around each other growing up. He'd seen her at school dances, home games, a few county fairs, with her always amid a group of girls and him hanging out with his teammates. He'd never been near enough to give her anything she could consider encouragement.

And a schoolgirl crush wasn't love.

She had convinced herself it was…

Or maybe she just wanted to convince *him*.

That come-on the other day, her hand outstretched in invitation, her shy admission she had "waited" for him…

All right, yeah, she might have waited. But once she'd satisfied her schoolgirl fantasy of him being her first, would she stay?

Neither his luck nor his prior experience gave him an answer he liked.

He wiped his forehead with the back of his hand and took a long swallow of his beer. Across the yard, the wrangler tipped his hat to Ally, and she laughed and made a little curtsy in farewell. That was his flirty Ally…

Damn.

She wasn't *his* Ally.

He needed to stop thinking like that, to stop thinking of all he saw in her. She was bold and flirty and quiet and sweet and made him laugh and turned him on.

But as he'd already proved, when it came to reading women, he had lousy eyesight.

Chapter Fourteen

Ally took a seat on one of the many wooden picnic benches scattered on this side of the Hitching Post's backyard.

Once Jed had announced the barbecue was done to perfection, he called the crowd to order. The hotel guests, the ranch's wranglers and the Garland family all lined up, plates in hand and—as their host said—appetites at the ready.

They had their choice of beef or ribs, or both, served right from a carving board set beside the barbecue. Slow-cooked beans came straight from the pot that had been suspended over the fire. Corn and biscuits and salads and big bowls of chile relleno, one of Paz's specialties, were all brought out from the hotel.

"Grandpa Jed makes the bestest barbecue," Tina and Cole's son, Robbie, announced.

"He sure does," Ally agreed. "And Paz makes the bestest chile relleno."

Everyone had mingled in the yard until the barbecue was ready, then carried their full plates to the long wooden picnic benches. As usual at gatherings here, or anywhere in her experience, the men gravitated to one area and the women and kids to another.

Ally would have liked to take a place beside Reagan. But at least from where she was seated, she could see him at the next table and overhear most of the noisy conversation that went on there. He sat a head taller than some of the men surrounding him, and though she couldn't fault any of Jed's granddaughters for their taste when it came to husbands, she knew which man she'd choose for hers.

She'd chosen him a long time ago.

At his table, Reagan fielded a few questions about what he had been up to since he'd left Cowboy Creek. None of his answers revealed anything he hadn't told her already. She wished Jed's phone call hadn't interrupted their conversation earlier. But still, the fact that Reagan had shared so much with her, painful as it had been for him, gave her hope their relationship had finally made a leap forward.

When the talk turned to his quitting sports after school, Cole grinned and said good-naturedly to him, "That gets you out of shape quick, Chase."

Reagan went right back at him. "We'll see how out of shape I am once we start throwing horseshoes after supper."

"Ally, you're not eating." Startled, she turned to find Paz looking at her, her brow wrinkled in concern. "I hope you're not having a touch of heatstroke."

"Oh, I think she's feeling the heat, *Abuela*," Tina said with a laugh. "But I'll bet it's got nothing to do with the sun."

Andi and Jane, seated on the same bench with Tina, laughed, too.

"No, it hasn't," Ally agreed calmly, "it's from all the luscious peppers in your relleno, Paz."

The older woman smiled. When she glanced away, Ally shot Tina a dirty look.

"Is there more biscuits?" Robbie asked.

"Yes, of course, there are." Paz reached for the empty basket. "I'll get them from the kitchen."

"I can go," Tina said quickly.

"No, that's fine. I need to check things in the oven."

As Paz moved away from the table, Ally turned to Tina. "Trying to run off, were you, *chica*? Thanks for the support a minute ago."

Jane laughed. "Give it up, Ally," she said, keeping her voice down. "Tina's right. If you'd been any hotter at that point, you'd have been breathing fire."

"Ally's a *dragon*?" Robbie asked in amazement.

"Yes," Jane said. "Ally's a-draggin' her heels over—"

"I am not," Ally insisted, rolling her eyes. "Jane's just teasing, Robbie."

"Nice teasing is allowed," Robbie informed her. "Mama says so."

"I'm sure she does," Ally said, flashing a glance at Tina, her so-called best friend.

She did trust that Tina wouldn't have shared anything they discussed in private, and that was all that mattered.

As for the other women, she had appreciated Andi's help with the crash course on babysitting, and so she didn't mind Tina's cousin knowing about her feelings for Reagan. But she hadn't realized their other cousin, Jane, had been let in on the news, too. She should have known. Family was family.

Besides, over the years, most of Cowboy Creek would have figured out how she felt about him.

All except Reagan himself.

Activity over at the men's tables caught her eye. The

sight of him rising to his feet made her heart beat double time. He was so tall, so broad-shouldered, so—

"Oops. Somebody had better grab a fire extinguisher," Andi warned. "Ally's ready to go up in flames again."

The three cousins laughed. Ally's pretense of glaring at them all just made them laugh harder.

Robbie turned to look across the yard. "Mama, can I go play horseshoes?"

"Ask Daddy," Tina advised. "It depends if the first game is just big boys playing, or big boys *and* little boys and girls, too. Daddy will tell you."

"Okay." Robbie swung his legs across the bench seat and jumped up to head across the yard.

"Ally, we know exactly which big boy you want to play with," Jane said. "And our teasing's just what you deserve, since you're always giving it to everybody else."

"Not everybody," she said with a grin. "Not *this* week."

The minute Jane left to get a pitcher of sweet tea for their table and Andi went along, intending to check on the sleeping babies, Tina turned to her. "Well?"

"Very well, thank you. And you?"

Tina sighed and shook her head. *"Ally."*

"All right," she said, still teasing, "then the truth is yes, you were right. I *am* feeling the heat. Maybe I should go lie down."

"Stop," Tina hissed. "What's going on?"

At her friend's suddenly serious expression, Ally sobered, too. She sighed, but not in pretend exasperation as Tina had a moment ago. More with a mixture of equal parts frustration and confusion.

"Things are going…better," she said cautiously.

She glanced across the yard. Over near the barn the men were setting up teams for horseshoes. Judging by Robbie's wide grin, the little boys and girls were invited to play, too.

Her gaze drifted, casually she hoped, to the man standing beside him. As if he knew she was looking his way, Reagan met her eyes. She couldn't help smiling at him.

After a brief hesitation, he returned the smile, yet his expression looked strained. She felt the tiniest ripple of unease. A silly reaction, considering he'd been fine on the drive over here.

"Reagan is talking to me a little bit more," she told Tina, half as a way to reassure herself there was nothing wrong.

"That's good."

"But he has something bothering him, and he won't talk to me about it." He would have, if Jed's call this morning hadn't come at the exact time it had. Reagan would have made the decision to talk to her then. She was sure of it.

"He'll open up with you," Tina said, "sooner or later. You know what a talker Cole is and always has been. But you and I both know it took a while for him to let me in. Give Reagan some time."

"But that's just it. How much time will I have? At the house, we've started sorting some of his parents' things. There's a lot to go through, and I know he doesn't want to stir up all those memories. If he decides just to have everything hauled away or to drop it off for donation, he could be headed out of Cowboy Creek ten minutes later."

Unfortunately, even her logical, rational best friend couldn't argue with that statement.

As THEY CLIMBED the back steps of Reagan's house, Ally shot a look in his direction. It was almost dusk, with the sun sending out its last faint rays. His hair shone in the light, and when he swung open the kitchen door and paused to usher her inside, his eyes shone, too.

Smiling, she went past him into the kitchen.

"Coffee?" she asked. "Paz sent home some of her special almond cookies." *Home.* Wondering if he had noticed the slip, she tried not to wince.

He didn't answer. He was focused on unbuckling the straps around Sean, who had fallen asleep in the car seat on their way home... Well, it *was* Reagan and Sean's home. Until someone else bought it.

She swallowed hard. "I can take him up to change him," she said.

"No, I'll do it. Coffee sounds good."

She watched him go, holding Sean close against his chest. The sight made her heart melt. The thought that Reagan had wanted his child when the baby's own mother hadn't cared about him left her on the verge of tears.

She couldn't let Reagan see her like this.

After making the coffee, she carried a tray with two mugs and a plateful of Paz's cookies to the living room.

Reagan had sat here on this couch last night when he had told her about his ex. He'd been so hurt by the past, and she had been upset at hearing his story.

She didn't want either of them to have to relive bad times. And she had already acknowledged to herself that doing something twice—such as bringing him sweet rolls on a Saturday morning—didn't create a ritual. Yet tonight she hoped repetition would work in her favor. She hoped his knowing he had talked to her here and survived would make him feel safe enough to try it a second time.

A few minutes later, Reagan came downstairs and settled Sean in the playpen she had moved into the living room.

By then, she was curled up on the couch, ready and willing to listen to anything he would share. But something told her she would have to start the conversation rolling.

"Who won at horseshoes this afternoon?" she asked.

"Cole's team against mine," he said promptly. "Then Cole's again, then mine, and the final game was a draw."

"Must have been hard for you to lose, considering your school record and all."

"Don't you start, too," he said with a laugh. "Those guys weren't about to let me live it down because I'd quit playing after I left high school."

"Why did you quit? It's not like you."

His smile slipped away. He sat back and took a sip of coffee, cradled the mug in both hands and stared down at it.

Again, intuition told her she had hit on something. She had known whatever was bothering him was connected to the years he'd been gone. And since he had already told her about the situation with his girlfriend, there had to be more he hadn't shared with her yet.

"Couldn't afford to go to college without a full-time job," he said finally. "I worked nights, and that didn't leave me time for both sports and studying."

"But you were such a good athlete. And your grades

were good. I know sports are so competitive, but still..." She eyed him from under her lashes. He was still staring down at the mug. "I'm sorry you didn't get any scholarships."

"Didn't apply."

Her eyes flew open in surprise. "You didn't...not *anywhere*?"

"I didn't decide for sure to go to college until my senior year, and by then I figured it was too late to talk to my counselor about applying." He shrugged. "I already knew I didn't have what it took to go pro. I'm not complaining or trying to be modest, just stating a fact." He ran his thumb along the edge of his mug. "Besides, my parents were more important to me."

She frowned. "I don't understand."

"Yeah." He laughed shortly. "I heard that a lot back around that time." He glanced at her, then away again. "I held off so long about deciding on a college because my dad couldn't understand why I wanted to go away to school. We'd fought about it all through high school. I wanted to take college classes in ranching, ranch management, animal husbandry. And he couldn't see the point of that at all. He didn't know why I needed to go away when he felt I could have learned everything I needed to know about ranching right here at home. From him."

"And was he wrong?"

"Yes, he was wrong," he said with some force. "He knew a lot, but not everything. There are ways to make a working ranch and farm, even a small one, profitable. Ways to make the soil yield more plants—and healthier ones, to produce hardier crops. Ways to use technology to make a farmer's life easier."

He stood. For a moment she thought he planned to walk off, as if that was how he'd handled his emotions when he and his father argued.

Instead, he moved across the room to stand beside the playpen.

"My dad was old-school," he said, staring down at Sean. "And he worked the old-school way, which is fine if you're happy running a ranch that just makes ends meet. Don't get me wrong, we didn't starve, but there were only three of us in the family, and some months we'd have found it hard to feed a fourth."

He didn't say it outright, but she knew he was thinking of himself as a daddy, a *single* daddy, having a child to feed.

"But it wasn't just that." He turned to look at her. "My dad worked so hard. He couldn't afford help. And when I was only a kid having to go to school every day and involved with homework and sports, that left just him, working day after day, sunup to sundown. That's a rancher's life. He knew it. I know it. But there are farming methods available today that they didn't have when he started out."

"Reagan," she said quietly, "I'm sure your father wanted what was best for you and your mama and himself, too. He didn't want just to make ends meet. No father does."

He shrugged. "It was a pointless argument, anyway. We didn't have the money—would never have the money—to invest in the equipment we'd need to put all those upgrades into place." He sighed. "And even if we'd had the cash, my dad probably wouldn't have gone for it."

"That's understandable. Sometimes people get set in

their ways, and it's hard for them to change. What about Jed? He owns a working ranch along with running the Hitching Post. Tina's the bookkeeper and she's told me that the ranch has always done well.

"I'm not telling tales out of school," she assured him. "Everybody in Cowboy Creek knows Jed's the most successful landowner in the county. And they all respect him for it." She frowned, puzzled. "You would have talked to Jed. Couldn't he convince your father?"

He gave her a crooked smile. "That *would* have been telling tales out of school."

"No, it wouldn't, Reagan." She set her mug on the tray, then braced her crossed arms on her knees. "Jed and your parents were very good friends. He would have helped you out with this, helped your father understand, if you had asked him. Jed's so good about helping everyone. That's what friends do for each other. Especially in ranch country."

She smiled. "I might live in town and love the stores and restaurants and the dances at the Cantina, but that doesn't mean I'm clueless about the people who live out on the ranches and farms. It doesn't matter where any of us live, in town or outside it. Everybody in Cowboy Creek pulls together to help each other."

She waited for his response.

After the silence stretched on, she took a deep breath. "And that's why it hurt so much, isn't it?" she asked softly. "Your father couldn't understand why you wanted to go away to school. But you couldn't tell him your reason—that you wanted to learn everything you could about ranching so you could help him."

Not answering, he looked down at Sean again. But his face had flushed, telling her she had guessed right.

Her throat tightened, and she blinked away tears. "You wanted to make things easier for both your parents. But you never told your father that, either, did you? You let him think you were selfish, that it was all about you and what you wanted."

"He was a proud man."

"So are you. And a good son."

"Not in my dad's opinion." His eyes looked black and bottomless. "The day I left for school we had another fight. And he told me never to come back again."

His words stole her breath. She wanted to go to Reagan, put her arms around him and hold him close. The instinct that had guided her so far tonight told her approaching him would only cause him to back away.

He was a proud man, just like his father.

She stayed where she was and prayed she had made the right decision.

Chapter Fifteen

Reagan had known Ally would react to his statement just the way she had, with both sympathy and understanding. He could see the shock on her face, the horror in her eyes, and he could hear the truth in everything she'd said.

"You were right," he told her, struggling to speak past the lump in his throat. "I didn't want my dad to know my real reasons for going away to school. I'd set out to do the right thing, and everything came out wrong.

"By trying to keep things from him, I hurt him worse than if I had told the truth. I didn't understand that then. Even if I had, it wouldn't have mattered by that point, anyway. It was too late. We'd both said things we shouldn't have. And when he told me never to come back, I didn't say anything at all. I just left."

"He didn't mean it." He could hear the pleading note in her voice.

"He did mean it, Ally. He felt I was rejecting him and what he stood for, felt I was abandoning him and Mom, and he struck back at me. I didn't realize it till later—much later, after he and Mom were both gone."

After Elaine had walked out on him and his son.

He crossed the room and set his coffee mug on the tray. Hands empty, he searched for something to do with them. Knowing he couldn't go for what he wanted, couldn't reach for Ally, he settled for crossing his arms and looking at her over the coffee table.

He settled for ending this conversation and moving on.

"But you know," he said, "you were right about something else. I do have good memories to look back on, from before that time. As a kid, I practically grew up in my dad's shadow—literally—following him around the house and out to the barn. He was always teasing me about keeping up."

Better run those short legs around and make 'em grow, son. I'll need your help a lot out here once you get bigger.

"And Dad was always doing something with wood. A big part of a rancher's life is spent checking on the corrals and the perimeter fencing, making sure there's no damage that could injure an animal, no breaks that would give the stock a chance to become trapped or get loose."

Can't afford to have any of the herd run off or let any of the ranch go to seed. This will all be yours someday, Reagan.

He crossed the room to the bookcases and looked down at the ceramic dogs and horses Ally had dusted the other day. "Inside the house, as you already saw, he was always making something for me or Mom. These bookcases here, the display racks in the kitchen for her china, the shelves and the bedroom set in my room. In his own way, Dad was as much into handiwork as Mom was."

"And your mama made your quilt."

He turned to face her again. "My quilt. All my baby outfits. And my pajamas and my shirts for school. Costumes for Halloween. My first cowboy shirt and pair of chaps. She even made me a couple of cowboy hats." He smiled. "Vacations were few and far between, but when we did go away, I drew the line. Everywhere we went, I wanted an official souvenir T-shirt for my collection."

"And the mouse ears?"

He laughed. "Yeah. That year, I wanted the mouse ears, too. And my parents got them for me, though Mom probably could have made me some just as good."

"What about here?"

"What do you mean?"

"When you traveled, you wanted souvenirs. What did you want when you were home?"

"I wanted…"

This will all be yours someday…

"I wanted to work the ranch," he confessed. "Beside my dad. Beside my own sons someday." He said it with conviction, because he meant it. Working and sometime in the far future owning the ranch had always been his dream.

"Then how can you leave?" she asked. "Why won't you stay?"

He hesitated, but there was no point in holding back now. "It's not the same without them here."

"No," she said quietly. "It can never be. You're closest to your parents, usually, from the time you're born until you grow up and start a family of your own. The way you have with Sean. Of course you know that. Of course you'd be sad at the way things turned out with your father. But you have all those good memories of them both to hold you here."

Again, he had to think before he spoke. He'd already told her more than he'd wanted to. Not all, but more than felt comfortable. He would tell her only one more thing, only because she needed to know the truth. "After what happened with my dad, everything changed. And it never crossed my mind to want to stay in Cowboy Creek now that my parents are gone."

"I know," she said. "I'll be devastated when the time comes and my own mama and papa are gone. But I'll want to stay here, because I know I'll have support from my friends. From everybody in Cowboy Creek. They'll be there for me then. They're here for you and Sean now."

She smiled. "You have such strong ties to this town, so many people who care about you and Sean. Your parents' old friends, your friends, everyone at the Hitching Post. You won't be lonely, that's for sure. And you won't be sorry you stayed."

When he said nothing, she walked over to the crib and looked down at the baby. "It's not just you, Reagan. Think about Sean. This ranch is part of his heritage, one you'll pass on to him. And long before that happens he'll work beside you, just the way you wanted. Between the stories you'll tell him and those he'll hear from everyone else, he'll be able to get to know his grandparents."

She turned to look at him again. "If you take Sean away from here, the only way he'll know them is through you. You'd be cutting him off from so many memories others could share with him. From so many memories he can help you relive and he can *make* here—with you."

Her smile was soft and sympathetic. Happy and hopeful. Concerned and loving and kind.

He couldn't return that smile when he also couldn't offer what she was asking for. He had to give her credit. She'd taken a good shot at trying to convince him. But he'd managed to resist.

Shrugging, he said only, "Sometimes negative memories pack enough punch to eliminate the positive."

"Sometimes they do," she agreed. "And sometimes we have to punch back."

WHEN ALLY RETURNED to the house on Monday with Sean, everything was quiet. She called upstairs, but received no answer.

"Oh, well," she said, "your daddy must have decided to work outside in the barn again for a change."

After their talk on Saturday night, he had told her he would watch Sean himself on Sunday. He didn't quite meet her eyes when he said it. Then again, he didn't object when she simply said she would see him on Monday.

Considering everything he had shared with her, she could understand he would want some time on his own. After all, she had told him herself what a proud man he was, just like his daddy. And she knew he was dealing with both hurt pride and painful memories. She wished he would let her help him. But at this point, the intuition she had come to rely on told her it was better not to reach out.

"I think we'll just stay here awhile, baby," she told Sean. "We'll go out to the barn later. You're tired today, aren't you? You'd better have a nap." She wasn't avoiding Reagan. The baby *had* been groggy on the ride all the way out to the ranch. Mrs. Browley informed her he had been cranky the entire time he was at her house, too.

In the living room, she found the playpen close to the couch. She wondered what Sean and Reagan had been up to all day yesterday…without her.

"It was awful, Sean, I know," she told him as she settled him for his nap. "Every time I said something to your daddy, I could see the wall go up higher. It was a terrible story, a terrible thing to happen. You and he will probably talk about it someday. But until then, I don't want you to worry about it, you hear me?"

Sean didn't respond. He was already fast asleep.

Welcoming a distraction from her thoughts, she rested her hands on the edge of the playpen and smiled down at him. He was the cutest one-month-old she had ever seen.

No, closer to a month and a half now, she realized in surprise. Sean and Reagan had been in town for almost two weeks. "I hope you stay longer," she murmured to the baby. "I hope you and your daddy stay forever."

A loud thud came from almost directly above her head. She clapped her hand over her mouth to smother her startled cry. Then she realized there was no need. The noise from upstairs would have awakened Sean. She looked down. As far as she could tell, he hadn't even blinked. What had Reagan done yesterday to make the baby so worn out today?

And what was that noise?

Reagan hadn't answered her earlier, but he must have been in the house, after all. Maybe he had fallen. After a last quick glance at Sean, she rushed up the stairs.

"Reagan?" she called.

"In here," he said from the direction of his room. She frowned. His voice sounded thick and sluggish, as if he were as tired as his son.

She hurried the last few steps to his doorway.

He sat on the edge of his bed. At his feet, a cardboard carton lay on its side on the varnished floorboards.

"Are you okay? What was that noise?"

"Box fell," he said shortly.

Kneeling, she turned the carton upright. Only then did she notice he was focused on several sheets of paper he held in one hand. The white stationery was filled with neat, sloping handwriting in purple ink and embossed with a border of violets.

She knew what he was holding before he told her.

"From my mom."

On the bed lay a white envelope that matched the stationery, with one word written in purple across the front of it.

Reagan.

For just a moment, she closed her eyes, praying she would find the right words to say. When she opened her eyes, he looked dazed.

She rested her hand on his knee. "What is it?"

"A letter she wrote just before she died. For me to open…after she was gone." He gestured to the carton. "She…she wanted me to have these things for my family. For my future kids."

She blinked away the tears burning her eyes. "Do you want to go through them now?"

"Now or never."

His effort to act offhand while his voice still sounded thick from his own tears made her eyes fill again.

He knelt beside her and, one by one, began unwrapping the tissue paper from each item he took from the carton, creating a neat stack that grew and grew and grew.

All handmade items knitted or sewn with love and care.

Tiny hats and sweaters. Pairs of baby booties.

Nightgowns and pajama sets in soft cotton, some printed with hearts and flowers, others with cowboy hats and lassos.

Two small afghans in pastel colors.

A one-piece footed jumper in red cotton with white snaps and Baby's First Christmas embroidered across the front in white thread.

The lettering blurred as her eyes filled with tears again. She thought of Reagan's mama making all these tiny items for grandchildren she had known she would never see.

Swallowing hard, she stroked the soft material. "It's big enough to still fit Sean at Christmas."

He nodded. He set the tissue paper and the jumper on the pile. Then he reached into the box for the last wrapped item. Much larger than all the rest, the package filled the bottom of the carton.

It held a quilt made of large, wide-bordered squares. Folded as it was, she could see only a half dozen of the squares. They were all made from cotton swatches embossed with logos and pictures.

The Alamo. San Diego Zoo. Yellowstone National Park.

She gasped and, like the embroidery on the jumper, all the words blurred. "Reagan. They're from your souvenir T-shirts, aren't they?"

He didn't answer.

She sat silently, waiting as he refolded the paper

around the quilt and dropped the bundle back into the box. As he scooped up the orderly pile of tiny gifts and placed them on top of the quilt. As he rose to his feet and crossed the room to set the box on the desk in the corner.

He stood looking down at it, his back to her. "My dad never told me."

She swallowed hard, recalling what he had said on Saturday.

The day I left for school we had another fight. And he told me never to come back again.

"After your fight...did you talk to him again before you left for Houston?"

He shook his head. "My mom wrote to me. For a while. Till she got sick." He put his hand flat on the box. "Her letters stopped coming and I didn't know why, but I was wrapped up in studying and midterms and work. Before I had a chance to call, my dad contacted the school, telling them to inform me she had died." He turned to look at her. "You know I wasn't here for the funeral."

She nodded. Everyone in Cowboy Creek had known. To her knowledge, no one had ever learned why he had never come home.

"The notification arrived after everything was over."

Her breath jammed in her chest.

"I regret what happened between me and my dad," he said evenly. "Every day. But I regret that most of all. Because of me—"

"*No.* Not because of you." She went to stand beside him. "You said yourself, you were trying to help your father the way you thought was best. The way you thought would be easiest for him."

"Yeah. Well." His eyes looked empty. He stared at the box again. "I guess not telling me about this—or about my mom dying—was what he thought was best, too."

Her throat tightened. She could see how much he was hurting, and yet she didn't know what else to say.

She didn't *want* to say anything. She didn't want to comfort him with words. Just as she had on Saturday, she wanted to put her arms around him and hold him close.

The instinct that had guided her that night, telling her not to approach him, had gone quiet. Very quiet.

She wouldn't have listened now if it had screamed in warning.

She touched Reagan's arm, then reached up—way up—with both hands to rest them on his shoulders, the way she had done the day he had first kissed her. Only this time, she was going to kiss him.

She was. Not flirty Ally. Not quiet Ally. Just Ally. The one who loved him and always had and who wanted to give him comfort.

She stood on tiptoe, cupped his face, urged him down to meet her.

He slid his arms around her waist and tilted his head toward hers.

And suddenly, she was no longer the one kissing him. He took charge, took her mouth, reached up to slide his hand down her back, his fingers caressing her braid. An uncontrollable shiver raced through her.

He must have felt her tremble. His response came instantly, a heavy weight pressing against the top of her jeans.

He scooped her up as easily as he had scooped up the carton from the floor.

The bed stood only a few steps away. He set her down there as though she were something precious, something that might break if he didn't take care enough.

His mouth was gentle on hers.

At first.

By the time he undid her buttons and slipped his hand beneath her blouse, she was shivering again with desire and need and nervous anticipation.

She might have lost the initiative, might have given over control, but at that moment, nothing mattered.

Nothing.

Except that this was Reagan Chase. And he was going to make love with her.

Chapter Sixteen

Lying in bed with her eyes closed, Ally smiled.

Reagan had gone downstairs to check on the baby, and she now heard the padding of his bare feet as he approached her across the wooden floor.

"Still sleeping," he murmured, sliding beneath the sheet with her again. "How about you?"

She opened her eyes. He was propped up on one elbow, looking down at her. "Am I *still* sleeping? You mean you think I slept through any part of…what we just did?" Her face heated.

As if knowing the reason for her blush, he smiled and shook his head. "Ally. What am I going to do with you?"

"The same thing you just did a while ago, please."

Now he laughed. With his free hand, he picked up some of her curls and let them drift down to spill across her shoulder. "What is this? I take off that one tiny ribbon and quiet little Ally becomes the flirt again?"

"You took off more than just a ribbon," she protested.

"Well, don't give me all the credit. Seems to me I had a little help from you."

"You did *not*."

He laughed again. He had laughed a lot this afternoon. She had wanted to give him comfort, and it had led to so much more.

She rested her hand flat against his chest, loving the heat and the hardness and the strength of him. "You didn't have any help from me with your clothes, either. But I seem to remember you were eager to take them off."

He brushed her hair aside and pressed a kiss to her shoulder. "You made me that way."

She blushed again. She'd never felt more shy, more powerful, more happy than she did right now. "I love you, Reagan."

He stilled, looking down at her.

She smiled. "And I hope I can make you that eager again real soon."

He reached up to squeeze her fingers, then lay her hand flat on the bed.

"Don't worry if you're not up for it right now," she teased. "We'll have plenty of chances to try again. But for those future times, we'll probably need to get another babysitter."

It took her a moment to realize he hadn't responded. It took her another second to realize there was more space between them on the bed.

Reagan stood.

A dull pounding started in her temples. He was getting dressed.

This wasn't good.

"Reagan?" She pulled the sheet with her as she scooted back to lean against the headboard. "Where are you going?"

He turned to face her and zipped his jeans.

"Ally, I'm sorry." He shook his head impatiently.

"No, that's not what I mean. I'm not sorry. I don't at all regret what we did. But future times, trying again, that's not going to happen. I didn't mean for anything to happen this time."

She knew what was coming, knew she didn't want to hear it, yet couldn't catch enough breath to tell him to stop.

"I didn't intend to sleep with you. But I got carried away. Very quickly. And it was… You were…" He cleared his throat. "I'm glad I got to…to help you be able to move on."

Astonishment forced her choked response. *"Move on?"* Hurt and anger suddenly broke the tension locking her throat. "You can't possibly believe that's what this was about."

He glanced at the doorway.

He did believe it.

Tears threatened, but she willed them away. "Searching for an escape route now, Reagan? Looks like you're getting ready to move on, too. You're so willing to be helpful, explaining what this was to me. What was it to *you*? A roll in the hay? A slam-bam? A chance to let the girl finally get laid?"

"*No.* Stop. It wasn't that at all. It was… I was… I wanted to be your first."

"*Oh-h-h.* Well, thank you so much. Now that you've done me that great honor, if you wouldn't mind leaving the room, I'd like to get dressed."

"Wait—"

"As I just said, if you wouldn't mind leaving…"

Both to her relief and dismay, he turned and walked from the room.

She buried her face in the sheet that still smelled of his cologne and fought not to burst into tears.

"Don't look to me for advice when you start dating," Reagan muttered to Sean, who looked up at him from his infant seat on the kitchen table. "When it comes to women, you and I both know I never get things right."

In the couple of hours since Ally had left, he'd tried countless times to push away the memory of her shocked expression, her angry words, her tear-filled eyes. He had failed every attempt.

He'd had no better luck trying to forget his own guilt.

At the time she had left, knowing he needed to give her some space, he had taken Sean with him to the barn. But even from that distance he had heard the back door slam, her car door slam, the car's engine race as she drove away from the house.

He hoped she had slowed down once she reached the main road.

"You and I," he informed his son, "are going to be bachelors until you're forty."

His cell phone rang, and for a moment he froze. But if it had been Ally calling, even the ring would have sounded angry.

He couldn't blame her for that.

He couldn't keep beating himself up. Just as with his dad, he'd had the best intentions. He hadn't wanted to hurt her with the truth.

The phone continued to ring. Reluctantly, he answered it.

"Hey, Reagan. Cole here. A few of the boys and I are headed in for a night on the town. We want you to come along. It's Ladies' Night at the Cantina, and the guys sure don't like to miss one of those."

He didn't care to accept the invitation, but Cole's statement was enough to surprise a response out of him. "Why are you going? I thought you were a happily married man."

"I am. Nobody's happier than I am, believe me. But the boys twisted my arm." Cole laughed. "They need someone to keep them in line. We're planning to have supper there and a few beers. So, how about it? And I'm not taking no for an answer."

"Thanks, but I've got plenty of work to do around here."

"Work can always wait. It's not going anywhere, and neither are you, at least for a while, are you? Every man needs a night off."

Wasn't that the same thing he'd said to his dad over and over again?

Not that emptying closets and packing up boxes could equate to the long, hot, backbreaking work of running a ranch, but the principle was the same.

He sure as hell could use some time away from the house. The walls were closing in on him in a way they never had when he was a kid…when his parents were around. Sean could probably use the break, too. His daddy had been running off at the mouth to him way too often lately.

But he wasn't in a partying mood. "I doubt I could get Mrs. B to watch Sean at this late notice."

We'll probably need to get another babysitter.

He gripped the phone and swore silently.

"Didn't I say?" Cole asked. "Tina wants you to bring the baby over here. She thinks it's high time Emilia and Sean made friends. After all, if you change your mind and decide to stick around, the two of them will be school buddies from day one."

He hadn't thought about that. As a newborn, Cole and Tina's daughter was only a month or so younger than Sean. He thought of what Ally had told him about having good friends in Cowboy Creek. Sean couldn't get much closer to a friend than one a few weeks apart in age.

And he couldn't get much closer to an old school buddy and teammate than to have kids in the same class.

"So what do you say?" Cole prompted. "Are you in?"

The man's conversation would distract him. The night out would give him something to do besides spend hours thinking of Ally.

"I'm in," he said.

He hung up the phone and went to pack the baby's bag.

Again, he couldn't help remembering what Ally had said about folks in Cowboy Creek.

As far as he'd seen from the first day he'd dropped Sean off at Mrs. B's, his son had gotten along with his elderly caretaker. Otherwise, he wouldn't have left the baby there. And every morning he'd dropped Sean off at her house, he'd seen how much she had begun spoiling the baby.

Like the grandmother Sean would never have. He liked that idea.

Yet when Ally favored him…well, that was a different story.

He didn't want to think about why that was true.

He didn't want to think about Ally, period. But all day long, he hadn't been able to keep his thoughts from going back to what had happened between them this afternoon.

He'd made the right choice. Done the right thing. Been the right guy to be with her for her first time. Some cowboy she might know, some stranger she might meet—they wouldn't care enough about her to *be careful* with her.

But he...he cared about her. He cared enough to keep her from giving herself to just anyone and getting hurt.

He cared about her more than he should.

A couple of hours after she had arrived home, Ally eyed her reflection in her bathroom mirror. She had managed to fight off her tears but couldn't escape the heartache that had caused them.

She heard footsteps in the hallway and braced herself. Over her shoulder in the mirror, she saw a figure appear in the doorway.

"You're sure you don't want supper tonight, *querida*?"

"I'm sure, Mama. I'm going out with the girls."

"Is that a good idea? You don't seem yourself tonight. And you look feverish."

She shot another glance into the mirror. Her eyes and cheeks were still bright from anger and hurt and humiliation. She wouldn't need blush tonight but would darn well wear it, anyway.

"I'm fine," she lied, forcing a smile.

Mama nodded and walked away—exactly the way Reagan had done at his house.

All this time later, just recalling what he had said left her as devastated as when she had first heard the words. When she couldn't wait to leave the ranch. He'd at least had the decency to stay out of her way. As she

ugh the living room and kitchen, he and
nowhere in sight.

had wanted to *be her first*, as if it would
earn him a trophy.

He'd wanted to help her *move on*, as if she were just
one in a long line of women waiting for a turn to sleep
with him.

Eyeing herself in the mirror, she ran her hand
through her curls, scrunching and fluffing and making them look wilder than they ever had before.

The wildness made her think of what she and Reagan had done and how he had made her feel.

Her fingers trembled.

She reached for her makeup. Blush first. Mascara
later. Much later.

Every time she thought of Reagan she trembled
again, sometimes from remembered desire, sometimes
from fresh pain. He had ruined what should have been
the most special moment of her life to date. She had
given him her virginity—had given herself to the man
she loved—and he couldn't even admit he cared for her.

She needed to forget him.

In her bedroom again, she ran through all the clothes
in her closet, looking for the brightest, tightest, flashiest outfit she owned.

In these past few days, she had quickly learned so
much about herself. There were times she wanted to be
the quiet part of her personality and times she'd rather
let the fun, flirty part take center stage. Tonight definitely called for the fun, flirty Ally.

Fully dressed, she took a last look in her mirror. She
nodded in approval at her reflection before leaving the
room. But after taking a few steps into the hallway,

she paused, hesitated, then went back to open her jewelry box and grab the silver tassel necklace.

If she was going out to forget about Reagan, she was going all the way.

WHEN REAGAN ARRIVED at the Hitching Post, he saw Tina and Jed seated on the front porch swing. He parked in the lot for guests and carried Sean to the front of the hotel. He hoped he'd been right about this night out distracting him from thinking of Ally.

So far, it hadn't helped at all.

"Howdy," Jed greeted him. "I hear you're joining the boys tonight. That baby of yours might be a little young for the Cantina, though."

Reagan forced a laugh. "You know darned well I'm not taking him to the Cantina."

"Here, have a seat." Tina rose. "And hand over that little one," she added eagerly, reaching for Sean's carrier. "Robbie's all excited about having two babies to read to tonight."

"He reads to your daughter? At her age? I hadn't considered doing that with Sean." If he'd been around Tina and the rest of the Garlands more often, maybe he would have. "I'll give it a try. Over at the house, I just saw a box with all my old Louis L'Amours."

"Good choice," Jed said approvingly. "Start that boy off right with some Westerns."

"That's what I was thinking." Sean would enjoy hearing his daddy read aloud from those books. Judging by the way his son turned his head toward Ally when she sang to something on the radio, he liked being entertained. Or maybe he just liked Ally.

And how could Reagan fault Sean for that, when he felt the same?

"Well," Tina said, "Robbie's still learning to read, so most of the time he makes up stories from his picture books. But you know, that's a great way for him to use his imagination, too."

"Sure is," Jed agreed.

Tina took the baby into the hotel, and Reagan settled on the swing beside Jed.

"That girl's too modest about her accomplishments," Jed said. "Always has been. She's been reading to that boy almost since *before* he was born. She's not one to talk a lot about her offspring, either, but Robbie's smart as a whip, and that little girl of hers will be, too, if I say that about both of them myself. Which I have license to say because, of course, I've got granddaddy—and great-granddaddy—bragging rights."

Reagan laughed, then sobered quickly as he thought about Sean growing up without grandparents at all. That's what Ally had meant. His son could have those relationships right here. Jed and Sugar and Mrs. B and so many others in town had been his own surrogate grandparents, and they'd all be more than pleased, he knew, to stand in for Sean's, too.

Ally had also hit it right when she said it would be good for him to be around friends. He would learn things he'd never think of on his own. Things that would benefit the baby, like reading to him.

He wanted to do everything that was best for his son. As a single dad, he needed to make doubly sure he followed through on that.

As if Jed had read his mind, he said, "I'm sure you're a proud daddy when it comes to your son, too. You're to be commended for taking on the job of raising that baby on your own."

"Not much choice in that matter." He hesitated, not sure what else he wanted to say. But maybe because it seemed easier now he'd explained to Ally, or maybe because he felt his parents would have shared the truth with their old friend, he felt ready to talk. He told Jed about what had happened with Elaine, her refusal to raise the baby, the arrangements he'd made for her to give birth and grant him full custody.

When he finally fell silent, Jed said nothing for a long time. Then he clapped Reagan's shoulder lightly and said in a low voice, "You did the right thing, son. I'm proud of you, and I sure know your folks would agree and be proud of you, too."

Reagan squinted and looked out over the porch railing. In the fading light, he could barely see a thing beyond that point. "Thanks."

"It was a treat for all of us to get to see Sean the other day. He's a smart little boy, too."

"Yeah." Reagan cleared his throat, then said again. "Yeah. He is. Smart, and a happy baby."

"That means he's getting good care. From you, I know. And I'm sure from Ally, as well. Seems to me she's gotten all wrapped up in your son. And as far as I can see, the two of you have been building a solid relationship over these past weeks, too."

"She's Sean's babysitter, that's all," he replied, glad to hear he'd said the words evenly.

"She's more than that."

He stiffened. "What do you mean?"

"Well, right now, she's like me with my granddaddy bragging rights, isn't she? With all the time she spends with Sean and all the loving she's giving him, I'd say she's earned her mama's bragging rights, wouldn't you?"

"She's not Sean's mom."

Jed nodded. "I do know that. I'm using a figure of speech. And it's true in many ways. I saw her with your boy when you were all out here the other day. Believe me, she's gotten as close to him as a mama could have."

Closer than the baby's own mother had ever wanted to become. But even that was troublesome. "She shouldn't have gotten close—to Sean. He and I will be leaving soon."

"I know that, and she knows it, too. But I reckon it's too late." Jed eyed him. "You know, son, giving your heart to someone is always a risk. But as my three girls all have proven, the rewards reaped can be well worth taking the chance."

He'd taken that chance once already and, except for his son, he'd gotten little reward. He wasn't about to try it again.

Before Reagan could respond, Cole coasted his pickup truck to a stop beside the hotel.

Reagan jumped on board to join the other wranglers for their night on the town.

The ride to the Cantina was a loud one, filled with nonstop talk punctuated by laughter. Either Jed's men were a rowdy bunch to begin with, or they were all fired up about Ladies' Night. He felt sure it was the latter reason, judging by their good-natured competition over who was going to get lucky first.

That day Ally had held out her hand to him, he could have gotten lucky. He'd turned her down.

This afternoon, he'd had a special kind of luck. But

for now, for Sean's sake at least, it wasn't the kind that should be on his mind or in his plans.

He thought about what Jed had told him about taking chances and reaping rewards. What would he have said to the man if Cole and the boys hadn't come along and interrupted?

By the time they arrived at the Cantina, he still didn't know how he'd have handled his answer.

And when he walked into the bar with the other wranglers, he saw something else he couldn't handle.

Chapter Seventeen

The Cantina was packed to its wooden rafters, the noise level cranked up to ten times what it had been inside the pickup truck. Everybody was looking forward to getting lucky.

Yet as Reagan started across the crowded room toward the bar, he spotted the woman in the middle of the dance floor. Ally. She was laughing, being fun and flirty, wearing her bright clothes and makeup, her hair loose and wild.

His entire body jolted. It took a minute to realize he'd collided with someone whose bulk the football team would have appreciated on their line years ago. He and the other man nodded apologies at each other.

Reagan followed Cole and the rest of the wranglers up to the bar to get a drink. But, ignoring the possibility of another collision, he kept his gaze on Ally.

As she danced, he caught the glint of the shimmering necklace dangling above her low-cut dress. The front of his jeans tightened at the same rate his throat constricted.

He took a deep breath and let it out again, easing the muscles that were threatening to choke him.

There was nothing he could do about the jeans except hope no one else noticed. What the hell. He'd bet three-quarters of the men here were on the prowl and in the same state.

The music ended. Some of the couples drifted to the edges of the small dance floor. Ally and the man she was with moved toward the bar.

Her companion was the same wrangler he'd seen talking to her out at Garland Ranch. This close, Reagan recognized him as Wes Daniels's brother, Garrett. The other man hadn't ridden along with them to the Cantina. No wonder. He'd gotten here early to give his luck a jump start. Maybe he'd made arrangements to meet Ally here.

Maybe she'd already had her plans set with Garrett before she'd gone to bed with *him*.

And what if she had? He reminded himself he had no claims on her. She had no obligations to him.

But he also couldn't keep from kicking himself again for what he'd done. If he hadn't screwed things up so badly, he could've been the cowboy with her out there on the dance floor.

He felt something cold touch his shoulder. He turned to find Cole had reached back in the crush of people to tap him with a beer bottle. Reagan nodded his thanks and took the bottle. His gaze went right back to where it had been.

Ally and Garrett hadn't gotten far. Maybe deciding to wait until the mob at the bar died down, they had stepped over to one side of the room. Ally rested against the wall. Garrett had leaned his forearm on it a few inches over her head. Laughing and flirting, she lapped up the attention.

The fingers gripping his beer went numb, and he knew it wasn't from the ice-cold bottle.

He liked that laughing, flirty Ally. He liked the quiet Ally, too—the one who wore simple yet sexy blouses and braided hair restrained by a pale ribbon. He especially liked that she'd worn that braid for days, undoing it only to make love with him.

But then he'd made his mistake and told her the simple truth.

For the hundredth time, he assured himself his intentions had been good. He'd wanted to protect her from getting hurt.

Instead, he'd been the one to hurt her. And now he didn't know if he could ever make things right.

ALLY SMILED UP at the wrangler leaning too close to her, boxing her in. But that was silly. She knew the feeling came from her skewed perception. She always enjoyed chatting with Garrett out at Garland Ranch, and she'd hung out with him often enough here at the Cantina. It was only since Reagan had returned that her feelings about her sometimes dance partner…about any partner…had changed.

She had lost interest in every man in the place. Not that she'd ever had designs on any of them romantically. But tonight she couldn't even seem to enjoy herself on the dance floor the way she usually did.

The music started again, Garrett tilted his head, and she nodded. She was about to follow him when someone stepped up beside her.

Reagan.

He took her by the hand and went in the opposite direction, toward the side exit leading out to the Cantina's parking lot. She should have protested. She should at least have dug in her heels and made it more difficult for him to walk off with her like this. But she couldn't help wanting to know why he was here and what he wanted with her.

Outside in the lot, he released her hand when they reached a parked truck she recognized as Cole Slater's. She frowned, puzzled. He had leaned back against the pickup with his arms folded.

He said nothing. She was used to his silences but wanted more than that now. She wasn't about to let him drag her from the dance floor just to leave her standing here in front of him. "Well?" she demanded.

"You know what the guys in here tonight are looking for, don't you? You're too good for all of them."

Her mouth dropped open. She snapped it shut again. She tried not to think about the hollowness in the pit of her stomach. This was all he wanted? "I'm choosing to accept you meant that as a compliment, but I don't think I like where you're going with it. And it's none of your business, anyway."

She scanned the parking lot to make sure no one else was in earshot, then leaned forward and said quietly, "Sleeping with me once—or a dozen times—doesn't give you the right to decide who I can go out with."

"You're dating that creep?"

"You know Garrett's not a creep. And what I'm doing isn't your business, either." She forced a laugh. "I don't have to answer to you or anyone else, Reagan. I don't have to *be* anything to you or anyone. In fact, I don't even have to be *with* you anymore."

As sad as the words made her feel, as much as they hurt, she knew she'd had to say them. She needed to follow her heart—as soon as it finished breaking and she pieced it back together again.

She needed to tell Reagan a lot of things he wouldn't want to hear. After all the years she'd spent waiting for him, she owed herself that.

She only hoped she could hold on to her temper as fiercely as she was hanging on to her self-respect.

"You're the one who came after me tonight," she reminded him evenly, "not the other way around. I've got plenty of pride, you know. I'm done chasing you. I'm done waiting for you. I'm done being anyone but myself—no matter which self I choose to be." She laughed again, and this time she didn't have to fake it. "You know, it's ironic, but you were right. I can't keep my life on hold anymore. It *is* time for me to move on. To face the truth."

She edged closer to him and lowered her voice. "But what about you, Reagan?"

He shifted his feet, resettled his crossed arms. He wanted to run, but she would be darned if she would back away and let him off that easy.

"What do you mean?" he asked finally.

"It was obvious you didn't want me with Garrett— 'that creep,' as you called him. But you claim you don't want me, either. You can't face the truth. You refuse to see how much you're kidding yourself." Her voice broke. She had to wait a moment before she could continue. "All along, I've been honest about my feelings. About loving you. But you won't even admit you care."

"I've already told you the truth. I'm not getting involved or sticking around."

"You're still not hearing what I'm saying."

"Maybe you're the one not listening. Ally, I've been

clear about everything. From the beginning." He side-stepped and lowered his arms.

She hadn't realized how close she'd been to him, how much she had felt the heat of him, until he'd distanced himself from her.

He took another step away. "We... Considering how we left things today, I think it's best I pick up Sean from now on. I won't need your help with the baby anymore."

The glow of party lanterns strung around the parking lot burned her eyes. She blinked several times. Took a deep breath. Nodded. "Then give Sean all my love," she told him. "Since you don't want any of it, I have a lot left over."

Even as she turned and walked away with her head held high, the already broken pieces of her heart shattered.

She had waited for Reagan and loved him and made love with him. She had done all she could. And it wasn't enough. He was never going to wake up and see the truth.

EARLY FRIDAY MORNING, a few days after his trip to the Cantina, Reagan eyed the coffeemaker in frustration. He had never realized how slowly a pot brewed. Maybe it was more sluggish than usual this morning since he'd made this batch so strong. He would need the added caffeine to get him through the long day ahead. To keep him awake after his even longer night.

He'd had plenty of nights like that one in the past few days, but his mornings hadn't gotten off to such a fast and busy start until now, thanks to his boss.

He glanced down at Sean, lying in the playpen and looking as slow and sluggish as his daddy and the brewing coffee. "We're going to be a fine pair today, aren't we? At least at Mrs. B's, you'll get a chance to sleep."

Reagan would have to stay awake, which was why he'd need the strong coffee. He had to put in a lot of time on the road.

A lot of time in which most of his thoughts would be of Ally.

Still, the phone call from his boss this morning had given him a few other things to think about.

Like Reagan, the sales manager who handled New Mexico was on vacation. Lucky for the other man, he was in Hawaii. Along with some positive reinforcement—and the faintest hint of a threat about Reagan's dwindling vacation hours—his boss had convinced him to visit a potential and very promising customer.

"This is a big opportunity I don't want to miss," the man had said. "And you're right there, anyway. The client's in the far northwest corner of the state. Any man I could send would run up a few hundred miles. You'll be saving him—and me in the long run, since I pay gas bills for all my employees," he added pointedly.

"No problem," Reagan had told him, though it was more of a problem than it would have been a few days ago, when he'd had babysitting coverage all day long.

His day job wasn't one he might have chosen if life had been perfect, but life would never be that. Still, like his dad, he took pride in his work. And he needed to provide for his son. He had told Ally about the lean times, when his parents had struggled to put enough food on the table. He just hadn't mentioned how often they'd faced that situation. He would never let Sean experience that. Not if he could help it.

"Send me the details," he had told his boss.

Now the phone rang again. He frowned. The details were supposed to come by email, not phone. He checked the display. Recognizing the number on it, he immediately tensed. Was this call going to ruin his plans for the day?

He heard the worry in Mrs. B's gasped breath before she even spoke a word. "Reagan, dear, I'm so sorry to do this to you, but I won't be able to watch the baby today. I'm…um…indisposed."

He recognized the polite word for "feeling sick."

"That's okay, Mrs. B. You just worry about taking care of yourself. Get in touch whenever you're up to it, and meanwhile, I'll make other arrangements for Sean."

We'll probably need to get another babysitter.

Damn. The last time he'd replayed Ally's words was the afternoon when Cole had called to invite him along to the Cantina. What a mistake it had been to accept that invitation. But now, it made him think of Cole… and Tina. Tina would watch Sean for him.

As if she'd read his mind, Mrs. B said, "Jed said… I mean, I'm sure one of Jed's girls would be happy to sit with the baby. Here, I've got the number for the Hitching Post. Have you got something to write with?"

"Yeah." He dragged over the pad he'd used to take down some notes from the conversation with his boss. "Ready."

He got the number from Mrs. B, told her again to feel better and assured her he would call the hotel. He didn't have much choice.

He wondered what Mrs. B had meant when she started to say, "Jed said…" No doubt, he'd find out when he got to the hotel.

He had almost finished tapping out the number for

the Hitching Post when it occurred to him he could have redialed Cole's call from the other night. He hadn't heard from Cole since that evening. Oddly enough, he hadn't seen a sign of Jed Garland, either.

And, of course, he hadn't talked to Ally. He pushed that thought out of his mind and focused on his current disaster.

Even as early as it was, Cole would be out on the ranch already, working.

The way he would have been if he'd never gone to college. Never met Elaine. Never had Sean.

Regardless of all the bad things that had come of his decision to leave Cowboy Creek for school, he could never regret having his son.

The main number of the hotel was answered promptly by a voice he recognized.

"Jed, this is Reagan. Good morning. I've got myself in a jam here." Before the man could ask—and he *would* ask—Reagan told him the story. "So," he finished, "I was hoping one of your granddaughters could help me out."

"Well, I'm afraid a couple of the girls have gone off to Santa Fe for the day."

"At this hour?" he blurted.

"They're going shopping once they get up there, then for lunch and then more shopping. More than enough said, I'd reckon." The man laughed.

"Maybe I can try to contact Layne."

"Nope. Cole said she's headed out of town with her husband and kids, too."

He searched his memory. "How about Shay O'Neill?"

The man laughed harder. "Son, where was your head the other day when we were talking about her at the barbecue? She's not an O'Neill anymore, and she's just had three babies of her own."

"Right. Layne told me that. I forgot. Well, I guess I'll take Sean with me." Not the best idea. Walking into a potential customer's office with a baby in his arms wasn't going to make the client or his boss happy, which in turn wouldn't do much for his job security. Come to think of it, his son might not like it, either. They had both been up half the night, and Sean would need a few extra naps.

"You've got a long ride even one way," Jed objected. "And then you've got to drive back. Out in the hot sun all day long, that's not good for a newborn."

"Yeah. I guess you're right."

"I'm always right, Reagan," Jed said. "You need to give that some thought."

"I will."

"But don't fret. Tina's here."

"She is?" He hesitated. He *had* thought of her originally. "But she's got Robbie and a new baby to take care of."

"Don't worry, between Tina and Paz and me, we'll have plenty of folks pitching in to watch the babies."

"Great. Then I'll be there in about a half hour." He hung up the phone and turned to Sean. "Sorry to drop you off for the day, little man. But daddy's got a job—and a lot of thinking—to do."

About Ally.

Since their last conversation, he had sworn he would get this house emptied out and ready to sell and get himself out of here. Yet he hadn't made much progress.

His thoughts had been jumbled for days now, but every so often he'd get hold of a piece of something that seemed it might form a pattern, like the pieces of souvenir T-shirts Mom had cut up and turned into a quilt.

Slowly, much too slowly, he put all those pieces together and had finally come to his senses—about everything.

About those times he'd told Ally more than he'd intended to, more than he'd even realized he knew himself at that point.

Times he kept assuring himself he'd wanted what was best for her...he was only looking out for her...he didn't want her to get hurt.

Times he wanted her and told himself it was just about sex.

Times he made it clear he cared about her, but that was it...

Yeah, he'd come to his senses—a little too late—and realized what he should have understood a long time before now.

He did more than care about Ally.

A lot more.

REAGAN FELT EAGER to get on the road so he could get back home again.

At the Hitching Post, Jed greeted him and Sean and led them into the sitting room, where Tina's newborn lay in a portable playpen.

"You just put that little fella in with her," Jed said, "and the two of them will have a nice chat."

Reagan laughed. "I'm sure they will."

"I've got good news for you. We'll have an extra pair of hands around here to help out. Somebody who's got time off from her day job today. And she's been trained to work with kids, so you're all set."

"Great. What's her name?"

"Ally Martinez."

"Jed—"

"Son," the man said, as if he hadn't spoken, "whether or not you realize it, I'm doing you a good turn, something I venture to say you could use. I heard it looked like you two had words at the Cantina a few nights ago."

Jeez. The man had spies everywhere.

"But," Jed went on, "if this trip you're taking is important to you and you want your son in good hands, you shouldn't let your pride stand in the way."

I've got plenty of pride, you know. I'm done chasing you.

Reagan swore under his breath. If Jed only knew.

Heck, knowing Jed, he probably already did. Tina and Ally were best friends. What were the chances the conversation he'd had with Ally at the Cantina hadn't been repeated?

He heard the sound of the hotel's front door being opened and closed, then the tapping of footsteps in the lobby. Evidently, Jed did, too.

"If you'll excuse me…" he said hurriedly, not bothering to wait for Reagan's response before turning to leave the room.

The man must be expecting fireworks, or he would never have taken off in such a rush.

He heard the murmur of Jed's deeper voice and Ally's lighter reply.

Reagan looked down at Sean, now staring up at him from the playpen, his blue eyes half closed in sleep. "Hey, little man. You remember what we talked about the other day, about Ally not being your babysitter anymore? Just for today, it looks like you might get to see her again, after all."

Eyes open now, Sean kicked his legs and waved his arms.

Reagan wished he could feel half that enthusiastic about the conversation ahead.

Chapter Eighteen

Ally fully believed what she had told Reagan. She needed to stop putting her life on hold.

And yet four days later, when Tina had called her with the news of his request for a babysitter, her heart had given a little jolt. That didn't mean she wanted to see Reagan. Her wounded pride could take only so much, and it refused to allow her to run after him again.

But as unready as she felt to face him, once Tina explained the situation he was in, Ally couldn't say no to spending her day off at the Hitching Post. She couldn't turn down what might be her last time to see Sean.

When she crossed the lobby with Jed, he left her to go down the hallway to the hotel kitchen. She clamped her fingers on the sack from SugarPie's holding the sweet rolls she had brought with her. The way to a man's heart, as Mama and Paz would say.

She was beginning to wonder if Reagan had a heart.

Hers beat wildly as she stepped into the sitting room and met his gaze without blinking. Without saying a word.

He looked at her, glanced at the sack, then blurted, "It's not Saturday."

"No, it's not," she said coolly. "But having Sugar's

sweet rolls on a Saturday isn't a ritual with me. I can eat them any day of the week."

"Yeah, me, too." He shifted his key ring from one hand to the other. "Jed said you'll be giving Tina a hand with the kids. I was surprised to hear you were off for the day, it being Friday."

"I took a vacation day," she said evenly.

"Nice. My days are getting used up fast. That's partly why I'm working today."

He seemed rattled and definitely more talkative than usual. Ironic, considering all the hours she had spent trying to get him to open up.

"Well," she said, "I'm here now. If you'd like to get going…"

…if you wouldn't mind leaving the room…

How could it be that, only a few days ago, they had made love and she had been so happy and content, and then everything had fallen apart so quickly?

He turned to say goodbye to Sean.

This might be the last time she would see Reagan, too. Deliberately, she focused on his profile. Dark hair, blue eyes, solid jaw, strong shoulders. It was as if she were taking inventory at the store, making a list of things she needed to order. A list of things she just needed.

He was taking his time. Why didn't he leave, already?

As if he heard her thoughts, he said, "Maybe you'd better say hi to Sean before I go. He hasn't seen you in a while."

Her throat tightened. Her stomach did a crazy flip. She had been avoiding this moment, wanting to wait until Reagan was on his way before she approached the baby.

She joined Reagan beside the playpen.

Sean showed his excitement the way tiny babies did,

the way she had seen him do before, flailing his arms upward and kicking his feet in tandem. Her heart raced at the sight of him. Smiling, she leaned down to take him into her arms. She wanted to close her eyes and cuddle him close and inhale his fresh baby scent.

But not while Reagan still stood looking at her. "If you'd like to get going…" she repeated.

He nodded and unhooked a key from the ring. "In case I'm back late and you're able to take Sean home. I don't want to ask the favor, but—"

"No problem," she said briskly, taking the key and sliding it into the pocket of her jeans. "Sean would be better off going to sleep in his own crib. If it gets to be his bedtime, I'll make sure to take him home."

"Okay."

Still, he hesitated, seeming reluctant to leave. Or maybe that was her wishful thinking.

He backed a step. "You have my number if you want me for anything."

If she *wanted* him…

"We'll be fine," she said brightly.

He nodded. The second he went through the doorway, she cuddled Sean closer to her and kissed the top of his head. "Hey, my little boy."

Tears she'd managed to hold back till now flooded her eyes.

She loved this baby as much as she loved his daddy, and it was breaking her heart to know they were going to leave her.

IT WAS FULL dark by the time Reagan parked his truck outside the house. He crossed to the porch and went up the steps.

His day had gone on longer than he'd expected, with

traffic delays, a wait for the CEO at the client's office, internet problems when he was giving his presentation in the client's boardroom.

In the downtime, he couldn't keep from checking his phone in case Ally had left any messages. But he knew she wouldn't call. At the Hitching Post that morning, he could see the same determined, chin-up pride on her face he had seen in the Cantina's parking lot.

As he had all week long, he couldn't keep from thinking about her and what she had said that night—that he didn't want her flirting with the cowboy, yet *he* didn't want her, either.

If she only knew how wrong she was there.

And boy, if she only knew how wrong he'd been to do what he'd done this morning. She had been cool to him when he'd left the sitting room. He had stepped into the hotel lobby, then abruptly turned back, not sure what he was going to do or say. And he'd seen her kiss Sean and heard her talk to him in a voice filled with tears.

He couldn't deny the evidence of how much Ally loved his son. He had thought a lot about that today.

Now his hand shook as he opened the door.

The kitchen was deserted. No Ally. No Sean.

But from the living room he heard her singing to the radio. He smiled.

He walked slowly and quietly across the kitchen and down the hall. Not because he wanted to come up on her unawares to see how she was taking care of his son. Not because he wanted to startle her and hear her funny little screech. But because, though his feet were moving slowly, his heart was pounding and his pulse was jumping.

Because he knew his future and Sean's would depend on everything he would say in the next few minutes.

From the doorway, he watched her with the dust cloth, lovingly wiping each knickknack and putting it back on the shelf. He'd been too keyed up this morning to notice she had worn one of her bright blouses with all the colors, yet she had tied her hair back in the braid he'd gotten used to seeing.

His two Allys in one.

Sean sat in his carrier on the end table near the door. Reagan ruffled the fine wisps of his son's hair.

That morning, somewhere between leaving Garland Ranch and arriving at his destination, he had done a lot of thinking about what he'd heard and seen of Ally with Sean. And he'd finally managed to put all the last of his random quilt pieces into the pattern. He'd finally figured out why he hadn't let himself trust Ally.

It was all tied up in something he never let himself dwell on.

Feelings.

Feelings about his dad telling him never to come back. Feelings about his mom dying without him ever knowing. Feelings about Elaine deserting both him and Sean. Feelings that made him automatically include Ally in the same category as his ex.

He had been so wrong.

Ally wasn't at all like Sean's mother.

He had turned Ally away the time they almost made love—and she stayed to watch the baby. He made love to her then hurt her in the worst way possible—and yet this morning she had come to his rescue. She really did love Sean.

And she really did love him.

Crazy as it seemed, watching her so lovingly dust those knickknacks told him she really wanted to be there for the long haul.

So did he. He'd known that for a while but hadn't been able to admit it to himself.

Ally had been cool to him at the Hitching Post. Seeing her turn now and give him a blank-faced stare told him she was going to be cool to him again.

He'd messed up, hurt her, refused to believe her when she said she loved him. Rejected her after she had given him the gift of herself.

All along, she had been the one trying to win him. Now he had to apologize and win her, or he was going to lose her forever.

"Hey," he said, "I'm home." *Yeah, great start.*

"I noticed," she said.

"It's getting late. It's Friday. You probably have somewhere else you want to be tonight."

She shook her head. "No, I don't."

"Then maybe there's someone else you want to be with tonight."

She said nothing. He lost his breath, the way he had that time a wild kick on the football field sent a ball right to his chest. Only that didn't hurt as much as this did.

He glanced down at Sean and thought again of how much Ally loved his son. And how much she loved him.

Ally watched Reagan watching Sean. Her heart hurt and her feelings were all jumbled up, and she wanted to go to Reagan and tell him that no, there was no one else she wanted to be with tonight but the two of them.

She had already done her best, already given everything she could give. But she believed in herself and knew her love would win out over her pride. She wouldn't walk away tonight without telling Reagan again that she loved him. Because she did and always would.

But he needed to trust his feelings. To trust *her*.

And so, for flirty, chatty, teasing Ally, staying quiet right now was the biggest challenge she had ever faced. But she did it. Because she knew love could also win out over fear.

She dropped the dust cloth on the shelf and took a seat in the chair facing the door. Facing Reagan.

He brushed his son's hair with his fingertips. Then he took a seat on the couch. "I'm glad you could watch Sean today."

"You said that this morning."

"And I'm still glad."

She nodded.

"You're quiet tonight," he said.

"I can be when I want to be."

"So I've seen. You can be anything you want to be." He smiled. "And I can talk when I have to. When I need to. And I need to now. Ally…I'm sorry for acting like an ass this week, last week and ever since I got back. I've been gun-shy with you because of what happened with Sean's mother. And I have to confess, I used Sean as my excuse not to get involved with you."

She hadn't expected that. "Why?"

"Because I told myself I didn't want any short-term relationships or to have Sean get close to any women who wouldn't stick around. And while that's part of it, I realized there's more." He fiddled with a pile of magazines she had brought with her and left on the coffee table.

When the pile slipped from his hands to the floor, she swallowed the smile that hadn't yet made it to her lips. She went to kneel beside the coffee table to help him pick up the magazines. It reminded her of the day she had knelt beside him when he had unpacked the box from his mama.

The day they had made love.

As if he might have remembered that, too, he took her hand and waited until she rose to sit beside him. She would swear his fingers trembled for just a moment. Seeing him drop the magazines had already shown her how nervous he was. Reagan Chase never fumbled a ball.

She knew how hard it would be for him to share whatever he told her next.

She squeezed his hand.

He returned the pressure. "I didn't want to get close enough to another woman—to making a commitment again with another woman—only to have her walk away from my son. Or from me." He shook his head. "I think now I reacted to that the way my dad reacted to me, lashing out, feeling hurt pride, feeling rejected."

"I wouldn't have rejected you. I told you how I felt."

"I know you did. But I was…hell, I don't like to say the word, but I was *afraid. Was* afraid. I'm not anymore, Ally." He took her hand in both of his and pressed it gently between his palms. "I see how much you love my son. And how much you love me. I'd be a fool to give up a chance to be with the woman who has always loved me."

"Trust me," she said. "We're all fools sometimes."

"I do trust you. And I know you're one smart woman. You were right that night at the Cantina—I didn't want you with that cowboy. Because seeing you with him made me realize how close I might be coming to losing you. That's the last thing I want." He squeezed her hand between his. "I want *you*, Ally."

"Which me?" she asked archly, trying to hide her own sudden nerves. Reagan wanted her…but that could mean so many things.

He laughed. "I want both sides of you, Ally. The sexy, flirty woman in the bright colors who always makes me laugh. The one who knows how to get me hot, and who has me head over heels for her because I know, deep down, there's another side of her that's shy about many things."

He smiled and tugged gently on her braid. "And I want the quiet, shy woman who listens and understands and offers heartfelt advice but doesn't judge. The one who gets me hot, too, because I know what she's like when we're alone together." He leaned closer to whisper into her ear, "And it's damned sure not shy."

She laughed, even as heat flooded through her.

He wrapped his arm around her and held her close. "But mostly, Ally, I want all of you. The whole package. The sexy, flirty, quiet, shy, loving woman who had the patience to wait long enough for me to come to my senses. The woman who stole my heart and my son's.

"That night at the Cantina," he added, "you said I couldn't even tell you I cared. You were right. I couldn't. I don't mean I didn't care, but that I couldn't say the words. Now I'm saying it. I care about you, Ally. I love you."

A tear spilled down her cheek. He wiped it away with his thumb. Then he tilted her chin up and kissed her once, gently. "I'm glad you waited for me. I'm glad you never gave up."

"I couldn't," she said simply. "I've always loved you." She smiled through fresh tears. "And in case you're wondering, *my* heart has always been yours and Sean's to keep."

Epilogue

Four months later

From the corner of the Hitching Post's dining room, Reagan watched his wife flit around the room like a butterfly in her brightly colored dress. She was Ally today, as she was every day. Just Ally. A mix of many different women, and all of them his.

"That's some wife you've got there," Jed said to him.

"You're right about that." He had quit his job and come back home to run the ranch—where he and Ally would live and raise their kids. They had gotten married right here in the hotel last month, and the legal papers were in the works for Ally to officially adopt Sean.

He never would have guessed a few months back that his life could have changed this much this quickly. He had a few suspicions about how that had happened.

He looked at Jed. "I guess it's about time I thank you for the matchmaking services. You did a great job. There's just one thing I still don't understand. None of the folks at our wedding had ever heard about my place being up for sale this summer."

Jed frowned. "You don't say."

"I do say." He lowered his voice. "You never spread the word about the ranch, did you?"

"Well..." His old friend smiled. "The truth is, Reagan, you belong here in Cowboy Creek. Your folks thought so, too. They'd be happy with the way things have turned out."

He looked away. "I don't know. My dad...when I left..."

Jed rested a hand on his shoulder. "Your dad was a stubborn man at times, but he confessed to me he'd let his pride get in the way in that situation. He regretted what happened as much as you did and probably more. All you can do now is raise your kids on your ranch and pass on the good memories you have about your folks."

Unable to answer, Reagan simply nodded.

Ally came up to them and handed Sean to Reagan. Smiling, she said, "And what are you two talking about over here that has you both looking so solemn?"

He slipped his arm around her and kissed first his wife, then his son. "We were trying to figure out who Jed can match up next."

She looked at Jed reproachfully. "I thought you had saved the best for last! But you're still going to be at it, aren't you?"

"Well..." He gestured around them. Many of the couples in the dining room were together thanks to him. "Never say never." He shrugged. "Besides, you just can't argue with success."

* * * * *

*If you loved this novel, don't miss
Barbara White Daille's other books in*
THE HITCHING POST HOTEL *miniseries:*

*THE COWBOY'S LITTLE SURPRISE
A RANCHER OF HER OWN
THE LAWMAN'S CHRISTMAS PROPOSAL
COWBOY IN CHARGE
THE COWBOY'S TRIPLE SURPRISE*

Available now from Harlequin Western Romance!

Get 2 Free Books,
Plus 2 Free Gifts—
just for trying the
Reader Service!

HARLEQUIN® Western Romance

YES! Please send me 2 FREE Harlequin® Western Romance novels and my 2 FREE gifts (gifts are worth about $10 retail). After receiving them, if I don't wish to receive any more books, I can return the shipping statement marked "cancel." If I don't cancel, I will receive 4 brand-new novels every month and be billed just $4.99 per book in the U.S. or $5.74 per book in Canada. That's a savings of at least 12% off the cover price! It's quite a bargain! Shipping and handling is just 50¢ per book in the U.S. and 75¢ per book in Canada.* I understand that accepting the 2 free books and gifts places me under no obligation to buy anything. I can always return a shipment and cancel at any time. Even if I never buy another book, the two free books and gifts are mine to keep forever.

154/354 HDN GLPV

Name	(PLEASE PRINT)	

Address		Apt. #

City	State/Prov.	Zip/Postal Code

Signature (if under 18, a parent or guardian must sign)

Mail to the **Reader Service:**
IN U.S.A.: P.O. Box 1867, Buffalo, NY 14240-1867
IN CANADA: P.O. Box 611, Fort Erie, Ontario L2A 9Z9

Want to try two free books from another line?
Call 1-800-873-8635 or visit www.ReaderService.com.

*Terms and prices subject to change without notice. Prices do not include applicable taxes. Sales tax applicable in N.Y. Canadian residents will be charged applicable taxes. Offer not valid in Quebec. This offer is limited to one order per household. Books received may not be as shown. Not valid for current subscribers to Harlequin Western Romance books. All orders subject to credit approval. Credit or debit balances in a customer's account(s) may be offset by any other outstanding balance owed by or to the customer. Please allow 4 to 6 weeks for delivery. Offer available while quantities last.

Your Privacy—The Reader Service is committed to protecting your privacy. Our Privacy Policy is available online at www.ReaderService.com or upon request from the Reader Service.

We make a portion of our mailing list available to reputable third parties that offer products we believe may interest you. If you prefer that we not exchange your name with third parties, or if you wish to clarify or modify your communication preferences, please visit us at www.ReaderService.com/consumerschoice or write to us at Reader Service Preference Service, P.O. Box 9062, Buffalo, NY 14240-9062. Include your complete name and address.

HWR17R

Sage Lockhart and Nick Monroe are friends with benefits. When Sage asks Nick to make her dream of having a family come true, he agrees…only because he is secretly in love with her!

Read on for a sneak preview of
WANTED: TEXAS DADDY,
the latest book in Cathy Gillen Thacker's series
TEXAS LEGACIES: THE LOCKHARTS.

"You want to have my baby," Nick Monroe repeated slowly, leading the two saddled horses out of the stables.

Sage Lockhart slid a booted foot into the stirrup and swung herself up. She'd figured the Monroe Ranch was the perfect place to have this discussion. Not only was it Nick's ancestral home, but with Nick the only one living there now, it was completely private.

She drew her flat-brimmed hat straight across her brow. "An unexpected request, I know."

Yet, she realized as she studied him, noting that the color of his eyes was the same deep blue as the big Texas sky above, he didn't look all that shocked.

For he better than anyone knew how much she wanted a child. They'd grown quite close ever since she'd returned to Texas, to claim her inheritance from her late father and help her mother weather a scandal that had rocked the Lockhart family to the core.

She drew a deep, bolstering breath. "The idea of a complete stranger fathering my child is becoming increasingly unappealing." When they reached their favorite picnic spot, she swung herself out of the saddle and watched as Nick tied their horses to a tree.

Nick grinned, as if pleased to hear she was a one-man woman, at least in this respect.

He looked at her from beneath the brim of his hat. "Which is why you're asking me?" he countered in the rough, sexy tone she'd fallen in love with the first second she had heard it. "Because you know me?"

Sage locked eyes with him, not sure whether he was teasing her or not. One thing she knew for sure: there hadn't been a time since they'd first met that she *hadn't* wanted him.

"Or because," he continued flirtatiously, as he unscrewed the lid on his thermos, "you have a hankering for my DNA?"

Aware the only appetite she had now was not for food, she quipped, "How about both?"

Don't miss WANTED: TEXAS DADDY
by Cathy Gillen Thacker, available June 2017 wherever
Harlequin® Western Romance
books and ebooks are sold.

www.Harlequin.com